ALLSORTS

A Lockdown Writing Collection

JIM BECK
MARGARET DUFFY
LYNDSAY KELLY
CAROLYN MANDACHE
CLAIRE MILLER

Published in 2022 by Calum's Legacy Books

ISBN Paperback: 978-1-7397518-2-1
Ebook: 978-1-7397518-3-8

A CIP catalogue copy of this book can be found in the British Library.

Calum's Legacy Books is an imprint of Indie Authors World
www.indieauthorsworld.com

For Calum

About Allsorts

In April 2020, the early days of the global pandemic, Indie Authors World set up an online writing group to give people a creative outlet to help them cope with the seclusion of lockdown.

No one could have predicted at the time that there would be multiple lockdowns and a prolonged period of social isolation.

The initial purpose was simply to use writing prompts to encourage new ideas and stories. The writers had a range of writing experience from Jim who is a poet by nature — so prose was new to him — through to self-published authors like Carolyn and Claire. The weekly meetings began to take on a classroom feel. Led by experienced crime writer, Sinclair Macleod, the skills of the group grew as they learned a range of tips and tricks to help them improve their storytelling.

In June of 2021 we decided to put this book out containing a short novella from each of the writers. Money raised by the book will by used to support the work of Calum's Legacy.

About Calum's Legacy

Calum Sinclair Macleod died on 12th October 2007 after contracting meningitis. He was three months short of his 13th birthday. Calum was our son.

He was a bright, inquisitive, funny, kind and friendly boy who was loved by all those who knew him. We wanted to remember Calum in way that helped to express who he was, promoting fun, friendship and co-operation.

Through Calum's Legacy, Indie Authors World funded five young people aged 16–25 from Central Scotland to co-author, publish and print a book.

Now Calum's Legacy is starting on a new mission to find young authors who are struggling to have their voice heard in the tough world of publishing. Subsidised by Indie Authors World we will publish novels by writers under the age of thirty. This book will also support that work as all monies raised will be ploughed back in to help those young authors.

We hope you enjoy these stories.
Sinclair, Kim and Kirsten Macleod
For more information:
Instagram: instagram.com/calums_legacy/
https://www.indieauthorsworld.com/calums-legacy/

Acknowledgments

Our thanks to everyone who supported our project.

To each of the authors for supporting the group, their friendship, comradeship and encouragement throughout the time the group has been in existence.

Alasdair Currie of XYZ for the design of Calum's Legacy Logo.

Mixed Messages

Carolyn Mandache

Chapter 1

Where the Hell is my bloody phone? Sara thought to herself as she threw cushions on the floor in pursuit of her scarlet iPhone. Finally, it was excavated from the sofa, and she took a glance in the mirror, cringing at her untamed hair. No time now, she thought, my kids are taught not to be late, can't very well stroll in at half nine.

Sometimes she wondered if phones were a blessing or a curse, if she'd had a simple alarm clock, she wouldn't have been relying on the phone which seemed to enjoy hiding from her so much. Throwing the phone in her bag as she left the apartment, she was completely oblivious to the impact that little red gadget would have on her future.

Glasgow, New Year's Eve
The coins clinked as Andy dropped his spare change into the outstretched empty coffee cup. "Here you go, mate."

"Cold one the night, take care," Mark added, as he too dropped in some coins.

"Cheers guys, have a happy New Year", the homeless man replied gratefully.

They smiled at him, bundled in his sleeping bag against the harsh cold. It didn't seem appropriate to respond with the usual "same to you".

Sofia and the others turned a blind eye to the city's homeless. The girls were more concerned about their painful feet in heels as they walked to the Millennium Hotel, their home for the night.

They crammed in for a group selfie on the entrance steps, Sofia's slender sparkly arm outstretched to its maximum to fit them all in.

"I'll take wan fur yous if ye want?" offered the unfortunate man, already unzipping his sleeping bag with his frayed, holey gloves.

"No thanks, we're good." Sofia called back. "He'd only steal my phone anyway," she muttered to Becky as they headed into the hotel. Mark hoped the man hadn't heard her comment.

The hotel had hit the mark with the preparations for the festivities. The lounge bar looked beautiful; tastefully decorated with a toasty log fire burning, an ideal location for the Instagram photos Sofia and her friends valued so highly. He shook his head at their latest pose in front of the twinkling Christmas tree. Champagne glass in one hand they blew kisses to their numerous followers with the other. Sofia looked gorgeous as always, but her vanity and borderline obsessive desire for likes, retweets and God knows what else, was starting to bother Mark. Sofia beckoned him over, but he shook his head, preferring to chat to Andy rather than star in yet another group selfie.

"What's up Mark?" asked Andy. "You don't seem much in the party mood the night."

Mark nodded towards Sofia and her friends, "Yeah, I guess the constant photos get on my nerves sometimes."

"Aww come on Mark, Sofia's gorgeous. Wouldn't you want to take loads of pictures if you looked that good?" Andy joked, nudging his friend in the ribs.

Mark laughed. "OK maybe," he admitted, wondering if he was making a big deal out of nothing.

"Course you would! Anyway, it's nearly time for the bells... you up for some shots?"

"Sounds good, I'll meet you at the bar in a minute. Just need to send a quick text to Amy while it still works."

"That the phone Sofia got you for Christmas?"

Mark nodded, only too aware of the ridiculous amount of money it cost.

"Nice! OK, come over when you're done."

Mark fiddled with the phone, still not used to how it all worked. He hadn't imported his contacts from the last phone yet, but he knew his sister's number by heart:

> *Hey you. Can't believe It's a year since I saw you, I miss you more every day, even with all your annoying habits! Happy New Year when it comes, not the same without you here to celebrate xxx*

Edinburgh, New Year's Eve

Sara was wedged into the small couch between her friends Emma and Kelly. Sara glanced at Kelly's long, toned legs enviously, noting how she kept tucking her feet in towards the couch so as not to trip anyone up.

Emma swept her long fiery red hair over one shoulder and adjusted the straps of her dress for the umpteenth time. She was more of a jeans-and-T-shirt-type of girl, and being glammed up made her uncomfortable, despite the many compliments she'd received on her appearance that night. The small flat was crammed full of loved up couples and hopeful singletons. Laughter and a Chilled Ibiza soundtrack filled the air. Sara groaned as her friends made an escape bid, struggling to free themselves from the velvet cushions.

"Come on Sara, let's go and chat to those cute guys over there," Emma pleaded, trying to pull her from her seat.

Kelly grinned mischievously, obviously in agreement with Emma's plan. There were four guys, one of them was Sara's type, but she still didn't feel ready for dating any time soon, her friends just didn't get that. Flirting seemed to be so easy and natural for them. In contrast Sara always felt awkward when conversing with someone new. She hated the initial impression she felt she gave off... that she was standoffish, or worse, utterly boring. She was neither.

*

She had tried her best to make small talk, but soon Greg, the one she liked the look of, gave up. There were only so many one-word answers someone can take before the conversation inevitably died off. Sarah turned to the full-proof solution of every modern-day person feeling vulnerable in an awkward social situation; she pretended to be engrossed in her phone, finding something vital she had to read. Of course, it was an act, Sara viewed her phone only when necessary, she'd never been addicted like her friends.

Checking the time, she noticed it was nearly midnight, and her anxiety over the New Year kisses with strangers began to bubble up. She knew a few harmless pecks on the cheeks shouldn't bother her, she wasn't a prude, but her natural shyness made her hate the tradition. Sara's phone buzzed and lit up as a text message appeared. An unknown number, but it didn't take her long to figure out who it was from.

"Sara? What's wrong? You look like you've seen a ghost." Emma asked. The tall dark stranger she was talking to was momentarily forgotten as concern for her friend took over.

Sara said nothing and simply held the phone out to her two friends to read the message. It didn't surprise her that they jumped to the same conclusion as to the sender.

"Oh for fuck's sake! He's got some bloody nerve." Remarked Emma, blunt and to the point as always.

"Yep, he sure does" agreed Kelly. "Delete it now before I do!"

Sara pulled the phone away and tried to brush the text off as nothing, but knew by her thundering heartbeat that hearing from him still had power over her.

"I'm going to get a better view of the fireworks when they start, ok? See you in a bit" Sara hurried to the balcony, needing some time alone.

"Forget all about the text Sara, that eejit's not worth any more of your time" Emma called after her, hoping her friend would listen to reason.

With mixed emotions, Sara re-read the text. She'd grabbed a glass of bubbly on the way out and downed it, trying to settle her nerves. Joe's number had been scrubbed from her phone long ago, her brain trying to protect her heart. She gazed at the digits, trying to remember if they were familiar, but she wasn't sure. For all she knew, he had a new number anyway.

Is this who I think it is?

Sara stared at the screen, waiting for the message to change from delivered to read. Nothing.

Miss me more every day? Why did it take a year to get in touch???

"10, 9, 8, 7..."
The countdown had begun, and she half-heartedly joined in as Emma and Kelly appeared by her side and handed her another glass of bubbly.

"3, 2,1...Happy New Year!" the partygoers cheered, in perfect unison with the first golden fireworks lighting up the sky.

"To a fun, successful 2022" toasted Kelly, clinking her glass against Emma's and Sara's. The friends hugged, before moving around the room to share good wishes with other people. Sara's smile felt like a mask, as she tried hard to sound genuine, wishing all the while she could freeze time, block everything out, just for a few minutes, and make sense of Joe's message, and more importantly, how she felt about it.

Stealing glances at her phone between awkward New Year kisses, there was no reply. Sara grew more and more agitated as her suspicions were neither confirmed nor denied.

> *New Years' Eve bringing up memories? If you're who I think you are, I get that... we had some great times.*

Another few seconds with no reply and Sara regretted her moment of weakness in the last text. Why on earth did she give him the satisfaction of knowing that she still had fond memories of their time together?

> *You talk about MY annoying habits? Wow! Biting my nails and singing in the shower seem pretty tame compared to shagging someone else in our bed!*

Sara poured herself another drink, a generous vodka with a dash of coke, to try to settle her nerves. Emma and Kelly beckoned her over, and with one final text, she put the phone away; out of sight, out of mind... or at least she pretended that was the case.

Chapter 2

Mark woke up parched with thirst, his feet were cold, nothing new, since they were six feet five inches away from the top of his head. Somehow, they always found their way out of the bed covers. Sitting up, he groaned as the headache he'd hoped he would avoid hit him hard. Reaching for the glass of water by his side of the bed, he tried not to disturb Sofia, who was still out sound. They'd both been pretty drunk, the clothes scattered around the room evidence of their alcohol-fuelled passion. As he looked at the beauty beside him, Mark realised if truth be told, other than sex, their relationship had become pretty empty.

Wondering what the time was, he picked up his mobile. He yawned, 10 am was too early to be up, he'd only got to bed at 3, and not exactly straight to sleep. Noticing the text alerts, he smiled. He was looking forward to reading a reply from his sister and making a mental note to make sure they stayed in touch more often this year.

> *Is this who I think it is?*

Of course, he thought, she wouldn't know his new number yet.

> *Miss me more every day? Why did it take a year to get in touch???*

Mark's brows furrowed at that text, he hadn't seen Amy for a year, true, but they'd spoken on the phone. It wasn't the radio silence she was implying. He grabbed the luxury "His" robe from the back of the door and struggled to put the slippers on the right feet whilst staring at his screen. Quietly stepping into the lounge area of the suite, he sank into the plush couch, eager to read more from his uncharacteristically angry sister.

> *New Years' Eve bringing up memories? If you're who I think you are, I get that....we had some great times.*

Mark knew his sister had an odd sense of humour, but there was something seriously weird about the texts now. He quickly scanned the last message and realised there was no way those texts were from his sister. He laughed quietly to himself at the mix-up.

Mulling over how it could have happened, Mark brewed himself some coffee, enjoying the aroma. Checking the number with no alcohol in his system, he could see where the mistake had happened, a 3 instead of a 4, just one wrong digit and he now knew the innermost secrets of some poor heartbroken woman... or man. He settled in with his coffee and decided to offer some kind words to the mystery texter.

> Hey! You sent me some texts by mistake last night. Sorry your ex was such an arse....Hopefully this year will be a better one for you.

*

Sara, always a light sleeper, even with a hangover from Hell, stretched an arm out to reach her phone after the text alert woke her up. Her one-sided text conversation came flooding back to her, and she took a deep breath before opening the message. When she realised that she'd sent details of her trauma to a stranger, Sara felt her cheeks flush scarlet to match her phone.

Shit, shit, shit... she thought to herself, chewing her lip as she struggled to decide whether to reply or not. So the text hadn't been from Joe after all, which brought internal conflict too... was she relieved or disappointed?

> Oh my God! So sorry, too many drinks last night I guess....

She'd tried to keep it light and hoped the embarrassing episode was behind her. She shook her head as she dragged herself out of bed for a badly needed coffee. She pulled her long chestnut hair into a messy ponytail as she headed to the kitchen, and imagined what Emma and Kelly would have to say about the text fiasco. Most likely they'd find the whole thing hilarious and karma for replying to Joe at all. Catching a glimpse of herself in the hall mirror, she tried to wipe off the leftover mascara, and frowned at the freckles she was always self-conscious about, now visible without makeup.

A faint beep came from the bedroom, she put the kettle to boil and headed back to find her phone. It was another text from the mystery number.

> Don't worry about it, it happens to the best of us. How's the head this morning?

Sara couldn't help but smile at the kindness, easing her embarrassment instantly.

> Nothing a couple of Ibuprofen can't fix, how about you?

> Well I've felt better, I'll be honest, and will really have to wish a belated Happy New Year to my sister...who I thought was you ☺

Sara scrolled back to the first message she'd received, becoming aware that the only reason she'd jumped to the conclusion it was Joe, was because it mentioned not having seen the other person for a year. She felt foolish, more so as she cringed at her follow-up texts.

> Bet you'll be more careful with text numbers from now on eh? ;)

She knew whoever it was meant no harm, some friendly teasing, Sara played along:

> Likewise! Just imagine what you could have ended up sending to your sister!

At least now I can stop being paranoid that Joe was playing mind games with me... one romantic text and then silence.

> *None of my business of course, but this Joe shouldn't even enter your thoughts, no one deserves what happened to you*

Sara stared at the blunt text from a stranger, knowing it was true, but unable to stop the familiar pain stirred up by that awful memory.

The texts stopped for a few minutes, like an awkward pause in a real conversation, neither knowing quite what to say next. It's strange how social anxiety can even transfer to technology with a stranger, thought Sara.

> *Sorry, maybe I should keep my opinions to myself. If it makes you feel any better, having a few love life issues of my own....*

> *Oh really! Seems only fair you spill all then *taps fingers impatiently**

> *Guess so. Here goes then. I've been with my girlfriend since high school, always thought we were meant for each other. Now, not so sure, nothing really in common and she's changed so much.*

Sara was impressed by this person, who she now assumed was male, could open up so easily, with no hint of male bravado.

> *Don't get me wrong... she's gorgeous and the sex is amazing! ☺*

Sara laughed at the change in tone, before replying,

It's a cliché, but people DO change. Up to you to decide if you still love the new person she is....

That's true, still figuring that out. Speak of the devil...here she comes. Have a great day, things will get better. What's your name btw?

Sara

Good to virtually meet you, Sara, it's Mark

Chapter 3

"Right ladies, who fancies a mulled wine to heat us up?" Sara's dad asked as he spotted the steaming decorated mugs warming the hands of a crowd gathered around a nearby stall.

"Ooh, now you're talking!" Sara's mum replied, her cheeks flushed with the cold at Edinburgh's famous Christmas market. Schools wouldn't start back until the 6th, so Sara was pleased she'd arranged to meet her parents before the multi-national vendors headed back to their various homelands.

The market was crowded, and if hadn't been for the buzzing in her handbag, Sara might not have heard her phone as it beckoned for her attention. She used one glove-covered hand over her ear to try to drown out the background noise.

"Hello? Oh, Andy! Good to hear from you. Happy New Year...What's that you said?... Sorry, it's really noisy here, we're at the Christmas market. Can you text me instead?... OK great, bye then."

"I'm so pleased you two stay in touch Sara, it seems like only yesterday the two of you were splashing around in the paddling pool in the back garden!" Sara smiled at her mum's selective memory of her relationship with her cousin.

The two hadn't always been the best of friends, but she could admit they could always turn to each other for support. He'd even offered, several times, to go and beat Joe up when he heard what he'd put Sara through.

> How's the market? Better than the Glasgow one I bet! Who are you there with?

> Mum and dad, dad's gone to get us some gluhwein, it's bitter cold!

> Check you haha! Anyone else would just have said hot wine, but you have to use the proper name. Say hi to Aunty Jane and Uncle David for me

> Will do, what're your plans for today then?

Sara's dad returned with the drinks, struggling to carry three mugs. "Cheers!" they said, clinking the mugs together, enjoying the warmth and festive spices of the German drink.

"Andy says hi," Sara indicated the phone in her hand.

Her father let out a satisfied sigh after another gulp of his wine. "Not heard from him in a while, how's he doing?"

"Good, good, just having a quick catchup by text, too noisy to talk, I won't be long."

> First day back at tennis today, trying to shift some of the Christmas weight. Hopefully, McEnroe can keep his cool today...

"Any idea who someone called McEnroe is?" she asked.

"You've never heard of McEnroe?" her dad replied. "You cannot be serious!"

Sara frowned, wondering why her dad had switched to a dodgy American accent.

"We must be getting old David, people we assume everyone knows about are no longer hip and trendy!" Jane laughed before explaining that John McEnroe had been a very famous tennis player, and the American phrase her dad had used was his catchphrase. McEnroe's fame was founded not just on his talent as a player, but also for being a very sore loser and regularly challenging the umpire on his decisions.

*

Mark stuffed the towel and shower gel into his sports bag before reading the text from Amy. He hit his hand off his forehead, annoyed at himself for never sending a text to his sister, what with all the confusion. What was that girl's name again? Sara, that was it.

> *Amy! Happy New Year! Sorry, I could have sworn I did, but there was a mix-up with mobile numbers...funny story really*

> *Well, your funny story will have to wait. I'm dying to tell you some of the crazy "next big things" I've seen on DD. Top secret of course, as always*

Mark smiled, Amy loved to share inside secrets from being a runner on the TV show Dragon's Den. He was always under strict instructions never to tell anyone before the show aired, the way Amy spoke you'd think the phone would self-destruct after any info was passed on to him.

> *I'm on my lunch break, easier to text though, never know when they'll page me for something....the glamorous world of TV*

Mark scoffed, he knew that being a runner was anything but glamorous and hoped that Amy's dream of working her way up would one day work out for her.

> *Tell all then, what was it today? Chocolate teapot or something equally wacky and useless?*

> *There was this fancy robot that can cook burgers so restaurants can cut down on staff. All was going well until it went haywire and started flinging the burgers all over the place! The judges had to duck out of the way!*

Mark laughed out loud at the image in his head, never a dull day for Amy at work.

> *That sounds crazy Amy! Maybe the robots won't take over the world after all. I'm just getting ready to go play tennis with Andy, so I'll call you later ok?*

> *Yes, no problem, and remember it's just a game, I don't miss your childish outbursts on the court Mark ;)*

> *Haha, I'm sure I'm not that bad. Hope you don't have to chase after any more burgers x*

Mark grabbed his tennis racket and sports drink, ready to head out the door. He opened the small pocket in his sports bag where he always stored his phone, hesitating before he put it in. One last quick text before he locked up to see his friend.

> *Sara, hi it's Mark. Just wondered how you're doing? If you ever need to chat, I'm here.*

Chapter 4

Sara was very surprised to hear from Mark again, assuming that wrong numbers by text would have the same effect as wrong numbers by phone call... some embarrassment, an apology, and then back to life as normal, never speaking to the person again.

In fact, over the last few days, she would go so far as to say they had become pretty good support for each other. Sara knew her friends were sick to death of her harping on about Joe and what had happened. Somehow texting a stranger about it was quite therapeutic. Mark was sympathetic, a good listener, but also offered some really good advice. He had a wicked sense of humour, and never let their chats become too dark or depressing. He'd opened up more about the problems in his own relationship, and she hoped he'd found her own words of wisdom as comforting as she had found his.

Sara checked her watch and was surprised it was 6 pm, she had an hour to get ready for the night out she really could do without.

*Mark, been great chatting, but time's gotten away from me. I need to get ready, off to the launch of Skybar in Edinburgh, woohoo!! *cheers with zero enthusiasm**

Mark was surprised at how much time had passed too, he'd been texting with Sara for at least 2 hours and felt a wave of guilt, although he wasn't sure why. Sofia wouldn't mind, she wasn't the jealous type, or at least he didn't think she was. The opening of a fancy new bar would have been right up her street, he thought, the opposite of how it seemed Sara felt about the event.

Hey, I'm sure you'll have a great time, those friends you've told me about will make it fun I'm sure. I need to go too actually, off to The Ivy for dinner with Sofia. Been looking forward to it for ages, not exactly easy to get a booking!

Oh, lucky you! I've wanted to go there since it opened, let me know what it's like! I've heard the food is amazing. Have a good night.

You too, Sara, talk soon.

*

"Wow! This place is amazing!" Kelly exclaimed as she ducked under the lower branches of a beautiful artificial cherry blossom tree decorated with tiny white string lights. Sara waited patiently as her friends found the perfect filter to capture the tree looking its best.

"Cosmo?" offered a smartly dressed waitress, holding out a silver tray of liquid sunsets.

"Ooh, yes please!" Emma replied, delighted her favourite cocktail was being served free of charge. The three friends clinked glasses, and Sara had to admit the Skybar was pretty special. They found themselves a white leather rounded booth to sit in. The live DJ played some trendy background music, and although Sara had been in two minds about the night out, so far, she was enjoying herself as she caught up with what Kelly and Emma had been up to.

A man weighed down with camera equipment approached. "Girls, sorry to interrupt but can I just say... you're looking amazing! We're doing some publicity shots for the opening night. Do you mind if I take some photos?"

Kelly and Emma did not mind in the least, quite the opposite. Sara reluctantly agreed to the photos and awkwardly posed between her two friends, who seemed to make it look so easy. The camera loved them, and in Sara's mind, hated her.

"They'll be up on our socials and might be picked up by local media." Explained the photographer, glancing through the images on his digital camera. "These look great, have a good night ladies." He left them with a smile as bright as the camera flash.

"Wait a minute, what's the Insta account so I can look out for them?" Emma called after him, already opening the app. on her phone.

"SkybarEd, all one word, and make sure you tag us in your posts tonight ok?"

"Yeah sure, will do," replied Emma, a huge grin on her face from the excitement of not only attending the opening, but also lavishing attention; the free drinks, canapés, a professional photographer.

"Found the account, they have great posts, Emma." Kelly seemed equally enchanted with the vanities of the night, and Sara's earlier optimism that the Skybar opening night might be a fairly normal girls' night out was vanishing fast. She couldn't care less about bloody SkybarEd! Picking up her phone, she sighed, if you can't beat 'em, join 'em...

Hey Mark, how's the Ivy?

*

"Good evening, sir, do you have a booking?"

"Yes, 8 pm under Evans." Mark smiled at Sofia, he was really looking forward to the fine dining experience so many people would envy. Sofia smiled back, then withdrew her hand from Mark's, and turned her back to take a photo of the impressive entrance they had just walked through.

"This way please" gestured the waiter, introducing himself as Frazer. Mark, always the gentleman, called Sofia to lead the way, ladies first.

"Just a sec. Mark, the lighting's not great, and these flowers will look fantastic with the Mayfair filter. You go on, I'll meet you at the table."

Frazer smiled sympathetically as he began guiding Mark to the table. Clearing his throat, Mark felt slightly embarrassed that his date was more taken with the setting than the food of the infamous restaurant. He glanced back over his shoulder, and watched as newly arrived guests waited patiently for Sofia to take her perfect photo. Sofia's looks and charm would win anyone over, he knew there would be no complaints. He found himself wishing for a second, that someone would snap; that just for once, she wouldn't get her damn way.

"The menu, sir."

Mark took the leather-bound list, his fingers brushing over the gold-embossed Ivy lettering. "The wine list is at the back. Today's special is The Ivy Buchanan Street Fish Pie, which has lobster, salmon, scallops and prawns, served with spinach and encased in fresh puff pastry. Can I get you anything to drink at the moment?" The waiter's gaze flickered towards Sofia, clearly unsure if he should wait for her or continue.

Mark looked towards the entrance, Sofia did not look like she would be joining him too soon. "Yes, a bottle of Prose... No, make it a Merlot please."

Opening the crisp pages of the menu, Mark enjoyed reading the descriptions of the tempting dishes on offer, even though he had already decided on the Street Fish Pie. The prices were high, and as expected, he felt the familiar tightening in his gut and tried to ignore it. Often, he had to remind himself that he could afford luxuries in life, not feel guilt or worry, but elements of his adult lifestyle were so much of a contrast to his working-class upbringing, that he did sometimes struggle with how to handle it. Mark's phone buzzed with a text from Sara.

How's the Ivy?

Can't comment on the food yet, and my date is too busy taking photos to join me at the table!

He heard Sofia's heels approaching, put his phone in his pocket and smiled up at her. He tried to move past his annoyance now that she had joined him at the table, but it wasn't easy.

"What do you think? Worth the effort I'd say!" Sofia beamed as she proudly held the phone out for him to see the picture.

"Yeah... looks good I guess. Take a look at the menu Sof, I'm salivating just reading it!"

"OK, but you know I'll just pick my usual Mark, if they don't have it, I'm sure they can rustle me one up." Sofia closed the menu, barely skimming the sundry choices on offer.

"Your wine, sir. Would you like to taste it?" enquired Frazer as he showed Mark the bottle.

"No, no, that's fine, just pour please." Mark was always uneasy at that question, not considering himself any kind of wine connoisseur. Sofia frowned as her glass changed to crimson red.

"Sorry... I think you've got that wrong." Sofia looked at Mark puzzled. "We always order Prosecco."

"I thought we'd try something else tonight. I'll have the special please Frazer, sounds amazing. Sofia? Have you decided yet?"

Absentmindedly Sofia handed the menu to Frazer, speechless for a moment as she tried to process Mark's odd behaviour. Why had he ordered red wine? Mark always ordered Prosecco, he knew it was her favourite.

"Eh… nothing appeals to me on the menu, could I possibly have some grilled chicken, brown rice and green vegetables?"

Frazer smiled politely. "That shouldn't be a problem."

Mark sighed a frustrated acceptance, wishing he'd invited someone more adventurous when it came to food.

*

Sara was bored out of her mind, no amount of glitz and glamour could take away the fact that she wanted some decent conversation with her friends, a real social life, not a virtual one. Kelly had just about fallen off her seat in excitement when their photos finally appeared on the Instagram page. She and Emma were now obsessing over how many comments and likes the images gained.

"Do you think there'll be any more food?" Sara looked around Skybar hoping that something would soon do the rounds, food a bit more substantial than the beautifully presented, but tiny canapés they'd had so far.

"Not sure, grab some more cocktails, that will take your mind off it!" Emma drained the remainder of her mojito, the latest freebie they'd enjoyed. She raised her glass in the air and called out, "Excuse me, can we have 3 more please?"

Already feeling tipsy, Sara wasn't sure she wanted another, especially not on a relatively empty stomach. Every drink had been different too, a nice novelty, but she knew combining drinks would not end well for her.

> *Hope you're not still sitting on your own, although I might as well be! I'm being ignored for Instagram. Has your food arrived yet? I'm starving here…*

*

Mark's phone buzzed in his pocket, and although he usually ignored it on dates with Sofia, she never showed him the same courtesy. She was staring hypnotically at hers again, her practised fingers moved at an alarming pace as she typed up her well-thought out hashtags for her photos to gain the most views.

Reading the text, he smiled and couldn't help but sympathise with Sara. Sofia wasn't exactly proving fantastic company either and the tempting aromas around him were making his stomach growl too.

> *No food yet, and Instagram seems to be far more entertaining than me here too.*

Glancing up, it was clear that Sofia hadn't even noticed he was on his phone and it saddened him. This date was such a contrast to how it used to be between them. When they'd first started dating, and for a long time after, they couldn't take their eyes off each other long enough to even look at a menu. Their fingers would intertwine across the table, conversation flowed so easily. Mark barely recognised the couple they now seemed to be.

> *Maybe Sofia should have joined your pals and you could have come to The Ivy with me!*

That creeping sense of guilt came over him again, and he deleted the text, taking a large gulp of wine to help him relax. He'd been with Sofia for so long, he couldn't imagine anything else, and yet, this evening, which he'd hoped would be so special, was throwing a huge spotlight on their failing relationship.

Sofia lifted her glass, "Cheers Mark", they clinked glasses and Mark forced a smile as Sofia tasted the wine. "Urgh! You should have stuck to Prosecco, this tastes terrible."

On my fifth cocktail now and still only food in mouse-sized portions. Pretty soon I'll be up dancing and I am not a good dancer!

"Who's texting you?" asked Sofia, momentarily looking up from her phone.

"Amy." Mark lied, clearing his throat. "She's thinking of coming up to Glasgow soon and wanted to check I'd be around."

"Oh right, tell her I said hi."

Mark pocketed his phone, trying hard to think of something to say whilst Sofia continued typing, the clicking noise becoming more irritating by the second. He drummed his fingers on the table.

"So, how was work today?"

"Yeah, fine, a shoot for a River Island ad. Clothes were pretty decent and there weren't any bitchy models today, so that's a bonus."

There was another awkward silence as Mark waited to see if Sofia would return the question, ask how his day was, but that wasn't going to happen.

"I feel for Marcus and his mum, the clients I'm working with, the dad's pretty determined to get custody."

"Oh yeah, I remember you saying something about that before, I'm sure it'll work out." Sofia smiled. "Anyway, what kid wouldn't want to move to the States?"

Frowning, he wasn't sure if Sofia was serious or making a flippant joke, but to him, family law was never a laughing matter. He was passionate about fighting for the right outcome, especially where kids were involved.

A few more minutes passed until the food arrived. The presentation and aroma of his meal were amazing, but for some reason, Mark had lost his appetite. Picking at his food, he pictured Sara drunk dancing at a fancy Edinburgh bar and hoped her night would improve. To his amazement, he found himself willing his date to end, to escape The Ivy and have some time alone to think. Sofia slowly chewed her bland meal, barely making conversation at all, it seemed she was entirely oblivious to the enormous distance between two people sitting directly opposite one another.

Chapter 5

"Mark, I've made us some quinoa salad, are you coming to eat?" Sofia called from the kitchen.

"No thanks, I'll eat later, going through Marcus's family file to see if I've missed anything."

"Marcus? Who's that again?"

Mark sighed; more proof of how little attention Sofia paid to the things that mattered to him. "The 8-year-old who might have to go to the US, remember?"

"Oh yeah, well you can look that stuff over later, come and eat."

"I said I'd eat later." Mark shocked himself with his blunt tone. "It's not like the salad's going to get cold."

"OK, suit yourself."

Mark heard the chair scrape in towards the designer glass table and Sofia telling Alexa to play Capital Scotland to keep her company. The music drifted through to the lounge where he was working, he tried to block it out. The coffee table was covered in his notes as he pored over them, trying to find something he'd missed.

His phone buzzed with a text, and he shifted the papers around to find where it was buried.

So tell all, was the food to die for Mark? As predicted I did make a fool of myself on the dance floor and no doubt will never hear the end of it…I TWERKED mark…NO ONE should twerk!!!

Haha, I bet that was entertaining! The Ivy food was good, I think just too much on my mind to fully appreciate it that night.

Sorry to hear, hope all ok? You've been such a support to me, I'd like to return the favour…

A couple of things really, right now I'm focused on a custody case with an 8-year-old boy called Marcus.

OK, you mentioned you were a lawyer, didn't realise it was family law. That must be tough, the kids I teach are around that age, you get attached.

Mark smiled, this reaction was so much more on the same page as him. Professionally of course he was supposed to keep his distance, not get emotionally involved. Try as he might, he just couldn't do it, the future of that kid largely depended on him, and in some ways, he supposed Sara must view her job that way too.

His dad wants him to move to the States with him, trying to paint the mum as unfit, and I just don't buy it.

"Mark, can you paint the lounge tonight?" Sofia stood in the doorway, drying her hands from washing the dishes. "I want it all finished for Janey and Scott coming over at the weekend.

"I already told you, I'm working on this case tonight Sof." Mark gestured to the paperwork and could feel the growing familiarity of irritation toward his girlfriend.

"Surely you can take a night off, that case is all you seem to think about right now. What about me?"

Mark bit his lip, he didn't need a fight distracting him. "It's only Wednesday, I'll get the painting done by Friday, ok? Please, just let me focus on work right now."

Sofia's cheeks flushed with anger, like a spoiled child ready for a tantrum. Mark held her gaze, unwilling to back down. He realised how many times over the years he had given in and all the resentment bubbling under his skin.

"Fine, I'm going out for a run."

Mark forced a smile, "Good idea, it's a nice night."

Sofia stormed around the house making as much noise as possible as she changed into her sports gear before finally slamming the front door behind her.

Mark sank back into the couch, closed his eyes and tilted his head side to side to stretch out his neck and try to release all the stress and tension.

> *way. Had some kids go through hell with parents splitting up, if you can help avoid that then that's fantastic. Good luck!*

Sara's text was the motivation he needed, someone who understood the importance of his work. Sofia could pound the pavement and sulk all she wanted, Mark's focus was back 100%. Brewing himself a strong coffee, he settled back down with his paperwork, knowing it would be a long night.

*

Mark sat beside Karen Marshall, feeling almost as nervous as she was. The poor woman was shaking, unable to keep her hands still as she listened patiently to the judge running through the details of the case.

At the table opposite, in sharp contrast, Mr Marshall sat up straight in his designer suit, confidence oozing out of every pore, as if he'd already been told he would keep his son.

If that damned landlord had made sure all the security cameras worked Karen would never have been put through all this. Mark was furious at the injustice, anyone with half a brain would know that this loving mother, his client, would never leave Marcus alone while she worked a nightshift. He thought back to the interview with the family neighbour; someone Karen thought was a friend, her betrayal was unforgivable. It was no coincidence, he was sure, that she wouldn't look Karen in the eye, and now was noticeably better dressed than when he'd first met her. Mark was convinced Mr Marshall had provided a generous incentive for her to lie. Marcus himself had confirmed he'd stayed over with

Mary next door many times, but sadly too many adults, including his new step-mum, disputed the fact and made his account irrelevant.

Mr Marshall's generous donations to Marcus's school also created bias. The fact that Karen missed the occasional school event, or that Marcus was sometimes late due to her difficult shift patterns, was blown out of all proportion; twisted to make her look incompetent, when in reality her every movement was based around providing and loving her son.

Their pet dog had bitten Marcus when he'd wound it up too much, another point stacked against his mother. The fact Mr Marshall had bought the dog against Karen's wishes was not even considered.

"Having reviewed all the information, I am granting sole custody of Marcus Marshall to his father, Mr Stuart Marshall."

Stuart punched the air in victory, whilst Karen's heartbroken sobs filled the room, unable to control the emotional pain as reality sank in... that her son would soon live so far away from her.

Clearing his throat, Mr Carmichael had to raise his voice to be heard over Marcus's mother. "Mr Marshall can provide a financially stable life, with the best education, and Marcus will be able to grow up with his new baby brother. There is no other extended family in Scotland to help support Marcus's upbringing, so no family ties other than his mother..."

The judge continued his analysis of the case, but Mark and Karen were no longer listening, too shocked and disappointed to focus. After what seemed like an age, the ordeal was over. Karen mentally prepared herself to break the news to Marcus.

Stepping outside into the cool fresh air, Mark turned to his client, struggling to find the right words; "Karen... I'm so very sorry... Marcus should be with you."

"Just goes to show, it's true, money talks. Never would I have believed this could happen Mark, that my friends could throw me under the bus like this." Karen rummaged in her handbag, pulling out a compact mirror, "Jesus, look at the state of me! Can't let Marcus see me like this."

Mark watched her shaking hands dab at the streaked mascara on her face, feeling utterly helpless.

"Do you want me to help you tell Marcus?" The offer was made in earnest, but he was relieved when Karen turned it down.

"Mark, I know you did all you could. Stuart just has a talent at always getting what he wants."

Nodding in reluctant agreement, he drove Karen home and wished her well, and his involvement in the case was now over. Mark knew he'd have to work hard to stop the feelings of guilt and sadness he felt for this mother and son who would soon be ripped apart.

*

When he arrived home, he loosened his tie, kicked off his shoes and poured himself a large whisky over ice. Sofia wasn't home yet and he was glad of the time alone, to digest what had happened and try to somehow accept it. In his career, he hadn't lost many cases, and none had affected him as badly before. He crunched an ice cube, wincing at the sensitivity in his teeth, and yet somehow relishing it... a little pain for the hurt to

Marcus and his mum, which he felt entirely responsible for.

The seat vibrated beside him as a text arrived, he'd forgotten his phone was still on silent.

> *Hi Mark, been thinking about you a lot today, how did things go with Marcus and his family?*

Mark sighed and turned the phone face down. Somehow he couldn't bring himself to reply. He'd let down himself, Marcus and Karen already and didn't want to do the same to Sara. Pouring himself another generous whisky, he scoffed at how ridiculous that was, worrying about letting someone down he'd never even met? What was he thinking?

The phone buzzed again and it was dancing persistently across the seat now indicating a call instead of just a text.

Sofia's name appeared on the screen, he answered reluctantly.

"Hi, I'm on my way, can you put that Prosecco in the fridge to chill? The food's all prepared, I just need to heat it half an hour before Janey and Scott arrive."

"That's tonight?" Mark dragged his hand down his face in despair, entertaining was the last thing he needed.

"Well, yeah, it's Friday. Honestly Mark I don't know what's going on with you, did you forget?"

"Sorry Sof., slipped my mind. Can we rain-check? I honestly can't face it tonight."

"No Mark, we can't RAIN-CHECK. I've had a hard week; I want to relax with our friends."

"Oh, you've had a hard week? Sofia, will you think about that for a minute? You're a fucking model who's paid a ridiculous amount of money for looking pretty! You get pissed at me for forgetting about a meal with friends, but you've never even asked how my case went today."

There was a moment of silence before the phone went dead. She had hung up. Mark felt the anger ebb away, he knew he'd hurt her, but also felt a weight off his shoulder that he'd finally spoken up and made her face some harsh truths. Sofia would arrive home, they would open that Prosecco, cancel dinner plans and he would try his damndest to gently end their relationship, if she didn't beat him to it. A strange sense of calm came over him as he played it out in his head, momentarily blocking out the case. There was too much history between them for Mark to be able to switch off completely, he'd always love Sofia in a way, but he was grateful for the clarity he now had. Ten minutes later he heard her keys in the door. Time to face the music.

Chapter 6

Emma startled her as she knocked on the bedroom door. "Sara, are you ready yet? I know it wasn't a huge success with Graham, but I have a much better feeling about Nick. He's a hot junior doctor, I told you that right?"

"Only like a million times Emma!"

Sara sighed, thinking about the last disastrous blind date her well-meaning friends had set up for her. That arrogant idiot had managed to turn every single topic of conversation back to himself. It had been terrible, and she kept wondering if this was how Mark felt with his seemingly self-obsessed girlfriend, but then she felt guilty for judging, that was none of her business after all. Eventually, she'd used the classic going to the bathroom trick and fled the restaurant, she hadn't realised she had it in her!

Looking herself up and down in her full-length mirror, she smoothed her red dress down and ran her fingers through the loose curls she'd spent the last 20 minutes perfecting. There was another 20 trying to make them look natural and effortless. She knew she looked good, but in no way wanted this Nick guy to massage his ego by thinking she'd spent hours getting ready for him. The red lipstick matched her dress and shoes perfectly, but she wiped it off, and decided she was ready.

Emma smiled approvingly at her friend. "Wow Sara, you look fantastic and nice to see a bit of cleavage on show! Nick's a lucky man. The Uber will be here in a minute, I booked one for you in case you chickened out. You can thank me later."

Glowering at her friend, Sara tried to stay serious, but it was no use, that mischievous streak of Emma's always coaxed a smile from her. She pulled on her jacket just as the car beeped on its arrival outside her flat.

"If Nick's another idiot Emma I'm done with your matchmaking attempts, I mean it," Sara called back as she carefully took the stairs in her heels.

"Come on, think positive for once. This could be the night you meet 'the one'."

Looking over her shoulder, she laughed as Emma fluttered her eyelashes at her, as ever the romantic. "I've got my keys, so just pull the door shut when you leave OK?"

"Will do. I want all the details, Sara, phone me later, or tomorrow if you're otherwise engaged."

Sara smiled as she stepped into the waiting car. Emma loved to wind her up and although she was far from convinced these dates were a good idea. Her friends were genuinely trying to help heal her fragile heart and for that she was grateful. Taking her phone from her handbag, she was disappointed there was still no reply from Mark. The text she'd sent would be the last, for two weeks she'd persevered, ignoring the little voice in her head which kept reminding her he would have answered if he wanted to keep in touch. Self-doubt and a deep-rooted fear of rejection and hurt had taken over. Sara had convinced herself that the text friendship was clearly only of value to herself. Mark was probably glad to be free of her over-sharing, his good Samaritan duty complete now that she no longer spoke of Joe. Now she came to think of it, that was the first time in weeks her ex had even crossed her mind. Silently she repeated his name over and over in her head, surprised and relieved that the once familiar pain was no longer there when she thought of him. Putting the phone away, she vowed to at least try to give Nick a chance at dinner.

*

Sara played with her arrabiata, chasing the penne around the plate, feeling the strange, forced smile stretch across her face. He's very handsome, mum and dad would love you to date a doctor, she reminded herself.

"Would you think me greedy if I ordered a second main, Sara? I've skipped so many meals on my shifts that when I get the chance to eat properly, I go for it." Nick flashed a Hollywood smile and waited for her reply.

"No, of course not, go for it." She tried hard to think of something to say, she wasn't sure how many more medical horror stories she could stomach. Her red sauce was already resembling the blood and guts he seemed so eager to discuss.

Nick raised a hand to beckon the waitress over. "Can I have the same again please, and a double espresso too. Sara, anything for you at the moment?"

"No, I'm fine thanks." Such a strong coffee mid-meal would have seemed seriously weird normally, but since Nick had been stifling yawns since he sat down, it seemed a reasonable request. The long hours he claimed to work seemed humanly impossible. The coffee arrived first, and as he sipped the drink, he regaled yet another hospital story:

"Last week, one of the juniors was called into the surgery to assist with a bypass. The poor guy had been on for 24 hours straight and was meant to go home, but no, there he was, scrubbed up, scalpel in hand." After another sip of coffee, Sara squirmed in her seat, knowing from his previous recounts that pausing for dramatic effect was something Nick enjoyed. Set the scene before the full gruesome details were revealed.

"So, the surgery was going fine, until Sean, the junior, literally passed out from exhaustion. From what I heard; the ceiling was sprayed with blood as he clipped an artery when he fell. The poor guy came to a few minutes later horrified by what he'd done."

Don't say it Sara thought to herself, hoping he'd miss out his most annoying trait, the way he finished every recount of his medical career.

"True story."

Sara gave her shocked expression, well-practised throughout the evening, and wondered how many women he'd bedded with these stories meant to impress. Did they think of him as some kind of hero? Someone who could protect them in any situation? Nick was wasting his time if this was how he hoped to win Sara over. Always squeamish, she'd left high school biology class on more than one occasion due to nearly fainting. Tales from the ER were the last thing she wanted to hear.

"Anyway, enough about me, what about you Sara? I hear you're a primary teacher, you must have a lot of patience for that line of work." Nick tucked into his second plate of spaghetti bolognese; hoovering up the intestines that Sara now imagined the long pasta strands to be. She shook the image from her head and tried to grasp the opportunity to change the subject.

"Yes, that's right, primary 4. They have their moments, but mostly they're just a joy to be around at that age, and their imaginations never fail to amaze me." Sara felt her face light up as it always did when she thought of her pupils, she did love her career.

Nick nodded, smiling in agreement, Sara felt herself relax now that she was on safer territory for conversation. Maybe she was being too harsh, she should give Nick a chance. After all, those sky-blue eyes staring into hers were not only beautiful, they were also kind. Her mind began to wander as she pictured him in a white coat with impeccable bedside manner, a stethoscope draped around his really quite muscular shoulders. Feeling her cheeks begin to flush, she placed her chin in one hand to try to cover up the colour change. Never much of a flirt, she found herself gazing up doe-eyed at Nick as she waited for his reply.

"Yeah, you're right, that is a great age. A lad in primary 4 came into the ER just last week, maybe he was one of yours? He'd split his head open on the corner of a bench as he and his friends all tried to get out the school door at once." Nick swirled more spaghetti around his fork, taking another mouthful of his meal. The medical mishaps she could put up with, maybe. The deal-breaker would be those two words she couldn't take hearing again, and she willed that they would be swallowed down with his food.

"True story," he said, for the umpteenth time. Any attraction she had felt for Nick was gone just like that, cut out like a tumour, with those two little words.

Sara drained the rest of her glass of wine. "Nope, not one of mine, I'd have remembered that."

God, please let this be over! She thought and finally, it was. When Nick offered to see her home, she politely refused, breathing a sigh of relief as the Uber took her to her flat. He'd asked to see her again, which was awkward. She'd gone for the cliched excuse; that she realised it was too soon for her to date as she wasn't yet over her ex. To her surprise, those words no longer ran true, but at least it was an easy way out.

Kicking off her shoes as she arrived home, she took her boxed tiramisu over to the couch, curling up to watch some TV. The whole meal, she'd barely eaten, but she could never resist dessert, and had ordered one to go. Her appetite was slowly returning, and she savoured the first delicious bite as the TV came to life.

The first sentence she heard was, "Doctor, this girl's appendix will burst any second if we don't get her to surgery right away!"

Sara couldn't help but laugh at the irony as she quickly changed the channel and silenced the girl's cries of agony. She certainly would have plenty to tell Emma about her date, but it could wait till the morning. She'd let her romantic friend enjoy the possibility that she'd found Sara her dream man, before bursting her bubble... and banning her from matchmaking.

*

> *Sara, you up yet?? I can't wait a second longer.*
> *Give me a call!*

Smiling at her friend's optimistic impatience, Sara shuffled to the kitchen in her fluffy bunny slippers to make herself a giant mug of coffee and a slice of toast. Emma could wait a few more minutes for the gossip she so craved.

With an increased appetite due to lack of food at dinner, she enjoyed the satisfying crunch as she bit into the toast smothered with butter and marmalade.

She tapped Emma's number and was taken aback by how quickly her friend answered the phone.

"Well, how was it? I want every detail!"

"Nick loves being a doctor doesn't he?" she began, curious about Emma's thoughts on her observation.

"I guess so, just as well after studying all those years, but anyway, what about Nick? Super sexy right??"

"I admit, he's very good-looking Emma, but I better break it to you now, he's just not my type." Sara blew on her coffee, waiting for her friend's predictable attempt to convince her otherwise.

Emma's surprise was obvious. "What? My God Sara, he ticks so many boxes, what more could you possibly want?"

"Well, less hospital horror stories would have been good, I could barely eat with all the blood and guts he talked about. But moving past that, the worst thing was this bloody annoying thing he says all the time."

"OK. What was it that wound you up so much?"

"After every recount from the hospital he said, 'true story', it drove me crazy!"

There was a pause before Emma's reply, "Really? Something as small as that and you're writing Nick off? Don't you remember when Kelly went through her "amazeballs" phase?"

Sara laughed. "Oh yeah! Forgot about that, but that was different."

"How, Sara? She'd gotten into a habit of describing everything with that word. Yes, it was super annoying, but it wasn't like we stopped being her friend. When we told her it was driving us nuts, she stopped. The same would happen with Nick if "true story" bothers you so much." A hint of irritation had crept into Emma's voice, it didn't go unnoticed.

"Look, I'm going to be brutally honest here Sara. As much as I hate to say this, I think you're still hung up on bloody Joe, so no one measures up!"

"That's ridiculous, I haven't thought about him for weeks thanks to Mark." The words were out before she could stop herself, and with a sudden realisation, she admitted to herself that she was making silly excuses for why Nick was no good for her. The reason was not Joe though, it was Mark.

"Mark, who the Hell's Mark?" Emma replied.

Sara explained the whole text mix-up and how she'd come to befriend Mark, and now realised she had feelings for him.

"So, you've been like...sexting this guy?"

"What? No! Come on, Emma, you know me better than that!"

"You're saying that you've fallen for a random guy just by texting each other? Have you ever even heard his voice, or seen a photo?"

"No, just texts." Sara bit her nails nervously, feeling silly now, her cheeks burning to match the colour of the iPhone at her ear. Bracing herself for Emma's reply which would surely re-affirm how ridiculous the situation was, she was pleasantly surprised.

"Well, you have to meet him, Sara! This is too big a chance to throw away. What if he feels the same way? It's bonkers, but stranger things have happened!"

Sara beamed, a buzz of excitement went through her at the possibilities, but then she remembered the radio silence from Mark.

"I don't think that can happen, Emma, he stopped texting back about 2 weeks ago."

"There could be many reasons for that! Maybe he lost his phone, or someone died... or he's in hospital. You need to have more confidence Sara, not every guy's out to hurt you like that dick Joe."

Sara nodded, forgetting her friend couldn't see her down the phone. Deep down she knew what her friend said was true, but she also knew she wouldn't be able to send another text after vowing to herself that she was done. The chance of being hurt was too high.

She hung up the phone hoping that Emma wouldn't involve Kelly in her romantic confession. The two of them would continue to pressure her to contact Mark, and much as she wanted to, she knew she wouldn't.

Chapter 7

Mark sighed, he didn't want to socialise, but he found it hard to refuse his wee sister.

Mark was relieved, the October was one of the few Glasgow haunts he hadn't frequented with Sofia.

Amy was right about that; his mum was still in shock about the breakup. She kept pointing out he and Sofia were voted "most likely to get married" in the high school yearbook. Mark himself was not so broken-hearted, more struggling to accept that a relationship that had once seemed so perfect, and held so much history, was now gone. Combined with the Marcus case, it had all gotten too much, both his sister and his friends were increasingly concerned. The fun-loving, sporty, kind, capable lawyer was fading away.

"What's he saying, Amy? Any luck?" Andy asked, bringing her a cup of as she lounged on the couch. Mark's mate Andy was also a friend of hers, and she was enjoying a catch up with him.

"It's on! He'll be there, 7.30 October Café."

"Perfect, I'll text my cousin and tell her to bring her pals, as well as Barry and a few others. A proper night out is exactly what Mark needs, he just doesn't know it yet!"

*

He waited patiently for a reply, picturing his cousin debating whether or not to come out.

*

Mark got a long-overdue haircut and shaved for the first time in weeks. Looking in the mirror at his well-groomed reflection, he felt fractionally better than he had done recently. Amy was always fun, and when she teamed up with Andy they were almost guaranteed a good night out, double trouble. He still felt strange making an effort with his clothes and appearance when not to go somewhere with Sofia, but knew the October wasn't somewhere to show up in scruffy jeans and trainers.

Grabbing his keys, he checked his phone as he pulled the front door closed. There were no new texts, except for Andy to make sure he was on the way to meet him and Amy. In all honesty, he wasn't surprised that Sara no longer texted, and although he missed hearing from her, he felt he'd left it too long to spark up a conversation again. Pocketing his phone, he reminded himself that they'd never even met, and this connection he seemed to feel was ridiculous. I hope you find a great guy Sara, you deserve one.

*

"Mark! Over here, mate."

Looking around the crowded venue he spotted Andy waving to him from the bar. Mark rolled his eyes and groaned when he noticed that it was not just 'the three amigos' as promised, there was a sizeable group.

"We've just ordered a round, what can I get you?"

"Jack and coke, please."

Andy called the barman over and amended the drinks order, whilst Amy gave her brother her most angelic look. Her innocent face implied that Barry and three other girls being there too was a complete coincidence.

"I'm not buying it, Amy, this was a setup," he whispered. His sister's mischievous giggle confirmed he was right.

Andy returned his attention to his friends; "So, let me introduce everyone. This is McEnroe, my fiery-tempered tennis partner, our friend Barry, Amy is McEnroe's sister, Kelly, Emma and my cousin S—"

"That'll be £28.50 mate."

"Oh, right, there you go, keep the change. As I was saying—"

"You're McEnroe?" asked Sara before her cousin could finish, as she took her long vodka from him.

Mark was not thrilled at being introduced by his nickname. He cleared his throat before replying, "Guilty as charged, although I'm pretty sure Andy exaggerates, I'm not that bad-tempered on the court." He found himself struggling to tear his eyes away from Sara's to encourage Andy to back him up. They were an unusual shade of emerald green and he was shocked to find himself so instantly attracted to his best friend's cousin.

"No, you're right, you're not too bad," Andy finally acknowledged. He took a few sips of his pint before adding, "As long as you're winning!"

"Look! That booth's free, let's go!" announced Amy. She grabbed her drink and rushed over to the large table whilst it remained unoccupied.

"So, you're a personal trainer Barry?" asked Emma, hooking her arm through his on the way to the table. "I'm a PE teacher. Fitness is my life!"

Kelly and Sara gave each other a knowing look and smiled, Emma had never been backward at coming forward and it looked like there would be no complaints from Barry.

"After you," gestured Mark, discreetly trying to make sure he'd be seated next to the mystery girl with the long chestnut hair and beautiful eyes.

Sara scooched along to the end of the bench-style seat, pleased that McEnroe would be next to her. That doctor had been handsome, but this guy was an Adonis.

"You don't strike me as someone who would lose it over a tennis match," Sara observed as she stirred her drink with a stripy straw.

"Oh really? Well, appearances can be deceptive." Mark smiled and tried to remove his jacket in the cramped seat without bumping Sara to his left, or Amy to his right. "I've been friends with Andy for years, strange we've never met before."

"I guess that is a bit weird. We don't see each other as much these days, but he'll always be my favourite cousin."

"Really? The rest must be pretty terrible then!" Mark laughed then gulped his Jack and Coke.

"Hey! I can hear you two you know!" Andy complained in mock annoyance.

"Let me get a photo of us all, while we're still in a fit state!" Amy stretched her arm out, leaning back on her brother in an attempt to fit all seven in the picture. "Smile!"

The five complied and flashed toothy grins at the iPhone in the air. Mark and Sara both sighed heavily, then reluctantly smiled as they noticed the connection over their photo aversion.

"Are you from Glasgow Sara? Don't think that accent is from around these parts, am I right?"

"No, Edinburgh born and bred. Don't hold it against me, I know what you Weegie's can be like!" Mark was speechless for a moment as Sara's amazing smile lit up her whole face, she could have been from Mars for all he cared, he knew he wanted to get to know Sara better.

The chemistry between the two was not missed by the others around the table. Sara caught Kelly's eye, "he's so hot!" she mouthed, and Sara had to agree. For someone so good looking, she'd expected a massive ego, but it seemed Mark was unaware of how attractive he was, the same could be said for Sara.

Barry and Emma sat opposite them at the table, giggling like school kids; they'd hit it off straight away and Sara marvelled at how relaxed they were with one another when they'd only just met.

Reading her mind, Mark seemed to agree, "You think it's the drink or your friend's just found her soul mate?"

"Well, Emma is a notorious flirt, but I do think they look good together, and they're both annoyingly athletic. I'd give anything for Emma's legs."

"Your legs are pretty impressive too Sara."

Sara turned to face him, "How do you know? They're hidden under the table."

"Well, eh... I mean... I saw you standing at the bar when I came in." Mark played with the cardboard drink mats on the table, avoiding eye contact and looked uncomfortable. The shyness was unexpected, and to Sara, completely adorable. Such a well-groomed, outwardly confident man, and yet awkward in complimenting her. She decided to put him out of his misery.

"Thank you, McEnroe, nice to know you noticed."

That smile again. Mark felt his heartbeat quicken and found himself utterly smitten as the evening wore on. Sara was so kind and open with everyone around her, she barely spoke about herself at all, wanted to know more about the people around the table. Mark couldn't help but compare Sara's selflessness, to Sofia's selfishness. To be around someone like this, someone more like himself, felt good.

"Another round?" Andy stood up to head to the bar as Barry handed him some cash.

"Is this the fifth round already?" asked Sara, checking her watch. From experience, she knew she couldn't handle her drink too well and was determined not to make a fool of herself in front of McEnroe. She hoped he would ask for her number before the end of the night, it was so refreshing to meet someone who wasn't obsessed with talking about themselves, who could listen to others, and who happened to be drop-dead gorgeous.

Emma unlocked her lips from Barry's, winked across the table and said, "Time flies when you're having fun!"

Amy nudged her brother in the ribs, taking the chance while Barry was at the bar, to question him about the girl he'd been chatting up all night.

"You two seem to be getting along very well."

"Keep your voice down Amy." Mark urged

"Sorry, you know alcohol increases my volume. Anyway, she's a real looker and Andy doesn't have a bad word to say about her. For God's sake get her number!"

There was no point hiding it, the whole bar had probably heard Amy's advice, never mind their table. Mark cleared his throat, embarrassed. "Could you give me your number please, and not just because Amy ordered me to ask."

Sara beamed, secretly glad of his interfering sister as she wasn't sure this God of a man would have had the nerve to ask without being pushed.

Act casual Sara she reminded herself. "Sure, it's 07843 627 454"

"Ha! That's nearly exactly the same as my number!" announced Amy, listening in to make sure her brother would make the move.

"Can you repeat that please?" Mark looked up from the phone, it was far too much of a coincidence.

Sara repeated the number and he added her as a contact. One final test to see if his newfound crazy theory could be true.

"Let me phone you so you'll have my number on your phone too."

Sara smiled and waited for her manic robotic ringtone, the one she deliberately chose so that she always knew when it was her phone ringing; no one else would choose to have that sound.

The call came through and just as Sara was about to decline the call, as she only needed to store the number, she noticed something very strange. The screen said the caller was Mark. It took a second to register and then her eyes flew up to meet his.

"You mean that you, and Mark... the guy I've been texting for months, are one and the same?"

"Yes...and.... Andy's cousin, you are Sara?"

Sara put her hands to her cheeks in shock, while Andy tried to take in the discovery. The conversation died down around them as the others seemed to sense something out of the ordinary had happened.

"Right, spill Sara, you look like you've seen a ghost," ordered Kelly.

"OK, this is crazy guys..."

"What is? Come on, Mark looks pretty freaked out too. What's happened?" asked Andy

"Remember the text guy Emma?"

"Yes, what about him?"

"Mark is HIM!" Sara moved her arms up and down beside Mark, like some demented magician's assistant revealing a trick she hadn't prepared for, which was true in a way.

"Shut the fuck up!" said Kelly, her unique way of expressing disbelief.

Emma's eyes looked like they would burst out of their sockets as the penny dropped. "Wow! Like I said Sara, stranger things have happened, not sure when, but they must have."

"OK could someone please let the rest of us in on...whatever this is?" asked Barry, confusion was written all over his face.

Mark took over explaining the whole thing, from the text mix-up, to how the friendship grew, to the breakup and now this chance encounter.

"It's fate Mark, has to be!" offered his sister, positively glowing with excitement. He was not a believer in fate, but he was very happy with the way things were going.

The group finished their drinks and prepared to head home. Mark pulled Sara aside as they waited outside for taxis. "I knew I liked you from the texts Sara, but I didn't know I'd LIKE, like you." The two laughed at his childish joke, "Well, I LIKE, like you too Mark." Sara replied as they moved closer for the kiss that had been destined from the moment they locked eyes.

Chapter 8

"It's bloody Baltic!" Kelly shivered in her faux fur jacket as she got out of the car.

"Well, it is winter in the Scottish Highlands," Emma said as she closed her door and opened the boot to gather the three girls' luggage. Booked in for a week, they'd arrived in plenty of time to bring in the bells for 2023.

Amy's blue Beetle was already parked outside the picturesque log cabin and she flung the door open to welcome them, wearing an inflatable onesie, the product of yet another Dragon's Den failed pitch. "Who's ready to party?"

"What the Hell are you wearing?" asked Sara, laughing as she pulled her suitcase up to the house.

"Don't you like it? Damn, and I got you all one for Christmas. Joking! Come on in, the log fire's on."

"You better not get too close to it in that thing! You'll go up in flames!" warned Kelly.

Barry's Range Rover roared up behind them, making the girls jump as he beeped the horn.

"The gang's all here then?" Andy asked as he opened the back door.

Mark stretched as he got out of the car, his height always meant car journeys were a little uncomfortable. Sara had grown used to adjusting her seat any time she got in her car after Andy had been driving. He walked over and kissed her like he hadn't seen her in months, even though it had only been yesterday. One of the many reasons she loved him.

The friends settled in and at Sara and Mark's request, the phones were put in a "phone jail" only to be released just before midnight. Two reasons: they were determined this weekend would be quality time for the group of friends without staring at their phones, and no one wanted to see any more of Barry's private texts meant for Emma, but accidentally posted in the group chat.

With perfect timing, the first snow of the festive season began to fall in the afternoon, and the friends enjoyed a long walk in the forest as the wintery sunshine made the brilliant white snow sparkle underfoot.

"So, place your bets, will Andy finally make a move on Kelly tonight?" Mark and Sara held hands as they struggled through the deepening snow, looking forward to mulled wine when they returned to the cabin.

"Hope so, it's taken him long enough! They've been flirting for weeks, and I know Kelly likes him."

"It'll just be Amy left single then, I hope she finds someone soon."

"She didn't tell you? She's with the guy who designed that crazy onesie she's wearing. He couldn't come with her as he's got a big investor pitch tomorrow."

"Oh, wow! He must be a real catch!"

"Mark, be nice!" Sara laughed. "You never know, that onesie could make her a millionaire one day."

"Sure! So you two are best buddies now then eh?"

"I like Amy, yes, I wish she lived a bit closer."

Mark smiled, pleased Sara had bonded with his sister, Amy had never really taken to Sofia.

The afternoon flew by with games of charades, Twister, and an interesting game of truth or dare which resulted in Barry walking through the snowy local village in nothing but a bright green mankini. Emma was thrilled.

Everyone had brought something to contribute to dinner, and as they sat around the oval wooden table, they were all thankful to have such strong friendships full of fun. Both Sara and Mark found it hard to believe that one year ago exactly, their lives had been so different. Sofia and Joe were now ghosts, part of the past, but they were enjoying the present and looking to the future.

The girls headed to their rooms to get party-ready far earlier than the boys, and although Barry had offered to stay in the mankini, eventually they changed for the New Year celebrations too.

The cosy lounge featured huge windows to showcase the fantastic view outside. The friends settled into leather couches covered in fluffy blankets and took turns choosing their favourite music, playfully arguing over lyrics and making up their stupid ones too.

As it neared midnight, Mark seemed anxious that everyone took their phones back, and made sure they were charged.

"Amy, you know what mum's like, if she doesn't hear from us to say Happy New Year she won't forgive us till 2024!"

The annual countdown started on the TV, everyone counting along..."10, 9, 8, 7..."

Mark was determined to get the timing right but was careful not to draw attention to himself. The words were already there, he just had to hit send.

"3, 2, 1..."

Sara jumped as her phone buzzed in her hand, in perfect unison to the shouts of "Happy New Year!" around her.

> Sara, you are the best thing to have ever happened to me. Will you marry me?

> Yes

> This is Mark, right? ;)

Mark crossed the room, taking the ring from his pocket on the way. As he went down on one knee, Emma and Kelly squealed in delight, and Andy took the romantic moment as the perfect opportunity to put his arm around Kelly

"It's a perfect fit Mark, I love you. Thank God that you sent me that text by mistake last year!" Mark lifted Sara in the air and spun her around whilst their friends clapped and cheered.

"Right Mark, for sure mum won't talk to you till 2024 if she doesn't hear about this sharpish!" Amy warned. "And don't tell her by bloody text!"

TIMESLIP

JIM BECK

Chapter 1

"**A**re you one of these Time Travellers then?" the cab driver said to Alan Conway.

Alan opened his eyes. He had been dozing in the back seat after his flight from Glasgow to Boston Logan International Airport.

"Do you always start your conversations like that?" he asked.

"Nope," replied the driver," but you're going to the Eliot Hotel, and they're having a big meeting about time travel."

"I take it you're a believer in time travel."

"Well, let's say I like to keep an open mind on most things, you know, weigh up the pros and cons and reach a rational decision." Alan could see the driver's smile in the mirror.

"Okay then, how would you convince me that time travel was possible?"

"Well, first we assume that the current Space/TimeLine works linearly and that by using quantum mechanics it would be possible to build a machine that can travel forwards and backwards along this timeline."

"Where did you pick up this sort of knowledge, it's not the sort of thing I would expect your everyday cab driver to throw into the conversation."

"Oh, I just do this job to pay my way through University. I'm doing a Master's Degree in Nuclear Physics and Quantum Mechanics. You wouldn't believe how boring some of my drives are; the passengers are only interested in business, fishing, and pro-sports. It's refreshing to speak with someone who shares my interests."

They had a lively conversation, with Alan arguing time travel was not feasible, while the cab driver came up with alternative scenarios until finally they drew up at the hotel.

"Here you are, and thanks for the discussion, it was very enjoyable," said the driver.

Alan opened the door and paid the driver the fare, including a generous tip, he asked, "What's your name I might want to ask for you if I'm doing any touring while I'm here."

"It's Mac," said the driver. "Thanks for the tip."

"I'm Alan, and I thoroughly appreciated our talk."

Just as Alan was about to move away, Mac called out to him, "Sometimes you've got to look in the shadows to get a wider view of the entire picture."

The cab moved off into the stream of traffic.

What a strange thing to say, Alan thought, as he stood looking up at the Eliot Hotel. He picked up his luggage and walked up the stairs towards the swing doors into the reception area.

As he pushed through the tall doors with the brass handles and stepped inside, the first thing that struck him was the ornate chandelier, displayed in all its glory.

He noticed plaques on the wall, white with embossed brown shapes, to stand out. The walls were a cream colour, and the floor had a marbled surface, with light pink and white rectangles, and small brown squares at the intersections. As Alan walked up to the reception desk, an attractive young lady moved across to meet him.

*

Alan checked in, and a pleasant young man named Spencer escorted him to his suite and placed his luggage on the floor. After he left, Alan walked around the rooms.

There was a lounge, a bedroom with an en-suite bathroom, high-speed internet, and complimentary tea, coffee and biscuits.

The door to the bathroom led to a large bath with an impressive shower, and the obligatory toilet and wash-hand basin, and large fluffy white towels you might vanish in.

The lounge had two chairs and a couch, with a floor to ceiling window view looking out over the Boston skyline.

The bedroom contained an elegant double bed with a telephone.

Alan picked up his two cases and laid them on the bed.

As he was unpacking his luggage, he noticed that there was an unusual mirror in his room. It stood upright in an ornate walnut frame, with castors at the base to allow it to be moved around the room. When he stood in front of the mirror, however, he noticed there was no reflection.

What's the point in having a broken mirror?

Some feeling that he couldn't quite rationalise made him step through it.

I will need to phone reception to come and replace the mirror.

As he walked around the mirror and returned to the bed to continue unpacking his luggage, he found his cases had vanished.

Chapter 2

For a moment, he stood looking at the bed, not believing what he was seeing. A moment ago he had been unpacking, and everything was gone, including the suitcases. This was impossible, so what would be the rational explanation? First, he retraced all his steps through the rooms in the same order he had entered during his tour when Spencer had deposited his luggage but found nothing.

Alan felt himself getting angry. If this was someone's idea of a joke, he wasn't finding it funny.

He left his room, took the lift back down to the ground floor, and walked to the reception. He explained he was in room 415 and his luggage appeared to be missing. The receptionist, a different girl this time, moved to the keyboard and typed in details. "That's strange the system is saying the booking is for next week, it must be in error. I will arrange for a search in the hotel luggage area, and we will deliver your luggage to your room. I apologise about this."

He thanked the receptionist, and as he was moving back to the lift, saw a pile of papers on a table. He picked one and returned to the lift. As he was reading the headlines, he noticed the date was 27th July 2018, but that was 5 days ago. He wasn't impressed at the hotel leaving old newspapers lying around.

*

Back in his suite, Alan made himself a pot of coffee and again tried to solve this mystery by retracing his steps from the time he entered with Spencer. He visited each room in the same order until he was back in the bedroom.

As he was about to move towards the mirror, a voice came from behind him, "I wouldn't do that if I were you"!

Alan spun round in alarm. Behind him, a man had appeared that Alan had never seen before. He was over six feet, with a rugged build, black hair and cold black eyes. There was an air of menace that disquieted Alan.

"Who the hell are you? What are you doing in my room?"

The stranger sat down and gestured to a chair.

"Please sit down, and I will explain everything, although you won't believe me at first. You want to know why your luggage vanished from your bedroom, and maybe why the newspaper has a date 5 days in the past? What if I told you that both these things have happened because you stepped through the frame of what you thought was the mirror?."

Alan replied, "No way. There has to be a rational explanation."

"There is,," said the stranger," When you walked through the frame, you moved back five days in time.

That is because time travel is possible, and I will prove it to you."

Alan glanced to see how close he was to the door, and if he might reach it before the intruder caught him, but as he looked back the stranger smiled at him.

"I do not expect you to take my word for it, Professor Conway, but seeing is believing, as they say. I want you to walk through the frame from the other side and tell me if you see any difference in your room." Alan walked around the frame, stepped through, and looked around the bedroom. Everything seemed to be the same until he looked at the bed and, to his amazement, there was his luggage. He stood there for a moment, with his mind whirling as he tried to come to terms with the impossibility of what he was seeing. Suddenly he felt a cold sweat come over him, then he began having difficulty breathing. The room started spinning, then everything went black.

When he came to, he was lying on the couch. He glanced over at the bed and there was his luggage where he expected it to be.

Well, that was one weird dream.

"I'm going to have to give up smoking the magic mushrooms," he said to himself.

"It wasn't a drug-induced dream," said the stranger's voice from behind him.

Alan turned around and groaned with disbelief. "I hoped you weren't real."

"Your mind couldn't cope with what it was seeing, so you fainted. Don't worry though, it affects some people that way. Now, I know you will have questions you want to ask, and the group I work for is keen to meet you.

After you have been to the Awards Ceremony I will take you to meet them. They will be able to answer anything you want to ask."

The stranger walked out of the room, leaving Alan still stunned by what had happened to him.

Who was this mysterious group, and what did they want with him?.

He finished unpacking and storing his luggage. Then he went to the restaurant for a meal and a drink. As he was exiting the lift, he heard a voice call his name. Turning, he saw a friend from university, Derek Linklater. "Hi Alan, it's great to see you. Are you here for the Awards Ceremony?."

"Yes, if you're here for dinner, why not come and join me."

A waitress showed them both to a table, and they ordered drinks while scanning the menu to see what was available.

After the waitress returned with their drinks, Alan ordered a starter of king prawns, the main course of surf and turf, and finished with brownies and ice cream, while Derek had loaded baked potato dip, a main of porterhouse steak and fries, and finished with a strawberry rhubarb cheesecake.

"What's surf and turf?" Derek asked.

"Have you never tried it? Surf 'n' turf is the main course combining seafood and red meat.

Typically it's lobster, prawns, shrimp or scallops, which are grilled, breaded and fried and normally beef steak. I always enjoy it. You'll need to have a taste when they serve it."

"Thanks," said Derek, "I'll take you up on that." The meals arrived and were as good as Alan had remembered.

Derek had some of Alan's "Surf and Turf," and was an instant convert.

As they were lingering over coffee and mints, Derek said to Alan, "How are things going between you and Alison, is she still staying with you?"

"I'm afraid we split up last year, and there's not been anyone since. I have devoted my time to my work," Alan said.

"Sorry to hear that. I thought you two had hit it off together. Never mind, plenty more fish in the sea, as they say."

Oh, I thought I saw Tolka coming out of your room earlier. What did he want to speak to you about?."

At this question, alarm bells echoed in Alan's mind. He presumed Tolka was the man he had met in the room earlier? "Is that what his name was? He showed up and tried to speak to me. I must admit I didn't like the look of him, so I said I had to meet someone for dinner. He looked rather sinister, so I was glad to have an excuse to get away from him."

"So you didn't talk about anything?"

"No," said Alan, "I gave that as an excuse, and he took the hint and left."

After that, they spoke about what might happen at the awards tomorrow, asked the waitress for their bills, and headed off to their rooms. What Alan didn't know was that Tolka and another pair of eyes had been watching them while they were at the restaurant.

Chapter 3

The next day after breakfast, Alan went to the hall where the Awards Ceremony would occur later that evening. In the centre of the room was a raised dais with a large poster at the back, advertising The Hive Corporation, the sponsors of the event. Around the dais were several circular tables with six chairs per table. A lighting crew was setting up the spotlights, while sound engineers were positioning various microphones and loudspeakers. He walked over to the tables, where he met some other scientists who would receive awards at the ceremony. While they were there, a member of staff came up and handed each of them an envelope which gave them a copy of the award ceremony procedures.

As well as Derek, he met another colleague Karl Stepek who was also attending the ceremony.After talking to them, Alan returned to his room, where he watched some TV until it was time for the ceremony, then he headed back down to the Hall.

On arriving, he found chairs and tables set out with a list of who was assigned to each table. Fortunately his table was as the same as his friend Karl. As they were chatting, the lights dimmed, and the Master of Ceremonies walked onto the stage. "Welcome to the eighteenth Annual Scientific and Medical Research Awards, sponsored by the Hive Corporation."

There was a ripple of polite applause.

"Before we start, I would like to call on the following people to say a few words, because without their generous help and unstinting effort, this event would not be taking place. He then called for the CEO of The Hive Corporation, the Head of Faculty for Boston Sciences, and The Dean of Boston University."

There was applause after every speech, until finally everyone had spoken and the Master of Ceremonies returned to the stage.

"As you are all aware, several individuals are being recognised for their outstanding achievements in scientific and medical research. When I call out your name, please come forward to receive your award."

Alan listened to several friends being named until he heard his name called.

He moved forward, received his award, and gave a brief speech thanking those people who had supported him in the past year, then returned to his chair.

As the awards continued, suddenly the hotel plunged was into darkness. Initially there was a ripple of nervous laughter but as time went anxiety began to spread. Suddenly there was screaming and a cry for help, while others called for lights. Suddenly, a hand gripped Alan firmly by the arm and pulled him upright.

A voice hissed into his ear, "Quick, you've got to come with me right now. Hive has found out about our interest in you and is coming for you. You must leave now." As Alan felt himself being directed through the darkness, at first he resisted but the stronger the resistance, the more forceful the person became.

"Who are you? what's going on?" Alan said.

"Tolka sent me, quick, put these on, so you can see where you're going."

As the stranger thrust a pair of goggles into his hand, and Alan pulled them over his eyes he realised they were infra-red, and he could see shapes in the darkness. Then he was aware of another person behind him, holding his shoulders and guiding him through the crowd.

"Now quick, follow me," said the first stranger. "We need to escape during the confusion."

Alan was panicking, with his heart pounding and mind racing. Who were these people? Was he being kidnapped? Why should he trust them, and where were they taking him?.

He began struggling, he realised that he couldn't escape their grasp, so instead, he forced himself to relax in their arms as he followed them. He avoided people stumbling about in the darkness, or sitting in their seats too scared to move, but he was waiting for a chance to escape. As they dragged him down a corridor, he spotted a side exit out of the hotel and shook himself free from his captors. He immediately ran for it and shot out onto the street.

With the voices of his captors ringing in his ears, he turned right, and as he was running past a coffee shop, a hand suddenly came out and dragged him into it.

Chapter 4

Alan gasped in fright as Tolka dragged him into the shop and sat him down at a window.

"You are one lucky man," Alan said angrily as he recognised him." I nearly decked you there, never do that to me again."

Tolka looked at him for a moment "I'll certainly keep that in mind, but I wouldn't have recommended it.

Now look over there." He pointed at an occupied car parked across the street.

"The people in there are Hive members, who are waiting to take you to their offices." As they watched, Derek Linklater ran out the main entrance and sprinted up to the car. He had an animated discussion with the driver, then got inside the car and they raced off into the night. Tolka waved to the waitress and turned to Alan.

"We'll wait here until the car arrives to take us to a safe house, so we may as well make ourselves comfortable. Do you fancy a coffee?"

Alan was so stunned, he just nodded in agreement.

Tolka placed their order with the waitress, then phoned someone to arrange for them to be collected from the coffee shop.

After they received their order, Tolka took a sip.

"Mmm... This is fantastic coffee. I think I'll have a refill, and maybe a doughnut while we're waiting." Tolka seemed totally relaxed.

"Do you often do this sort of thing?" Alan asked.

"Not too often," Tolka replied with a grin. "Just enough to keep the job interesting. You and I will be together for the next few days, while you are introduced to the group, and we'll get to know each other pretty well."

As they both sat, drinking coffee and eating doughnuts, Alan looked around and thought, *Is this happening?. Maybe I'll wake up in my bed in the hotel room.*

About an hour later a car drew up, and Tolka said," Ah, here's our ride to the safe house."

As they were driving out of the city, Tolka turned to him and said, "The group you are going to meet is called 'The Guardians'. You already know about 'The Hive' as they have been sponsoring your work in proving that time travel is impossible, but what you are not aware of, is that in fact 'The Hive' has been working to achieve time travel, and has been successful.

"One scientist in their group was unhappy with their aims and reasons, and so he came to us to help us also successfully create time travel technology. With his help, we have also developed it, and a balance is now in place against what "The Hive" is trying to achieve.

The drove far out of the city, down winding country roads, before they eventually arrived at an isolated country mansion.

"Welcome to your new home," said Tolka. "I'm sure you'll enjoy your stay."

Chapter 5

s Derek was getting out of the car, his mind was racing. What on earth was he going to tell the directors of Hive to explain Alan's kidnapping? The directors expected Alan to be at Hive Headquarters that night for questioning. Had someone tipped The Guardians off? Why had Alan been speaking to Tolka earlier in the evening, and then he had dismissed it as a chance meeting when Derek mentioned it to him?. Why had Alan been so passionate about the impossibility of time travel if there was even the smallest possibility of involvement with The Guardians?

"The directors will see you now, Mr Linklater," said the butler, and opened the massive oak door.

As Derek stepped into the room, he felt a shiver of apprehension run down his spine, and sweat trickled down his brow. "Ah, Mr Linklater, do come in and take a seat," said a voice, velvety smooth yet underlined with threat.

The butler directed Derek to a chair at the bottom of a long table, where there were nine other men. Derek knew of them, all immensely wealthy and powerful, but the man at the head of the table had supreme control.

"You'll join us for coffee, of course," and the butler appeared at his elbow silently, with a cup of Kopi Luwak coffee, "And a cigar as well, perhaps?" said the leader, as he exhaled a cloud of expensive Cuban Havana cigar smoke.

"Thank you, Sir, but I don't smoke," said Derek, with a slight tremor in his voice.

"Excellent," said the man," They say smoking is bad for you, don't they." He leaned back in his leather padded chair.

"Now, I believe you have an explanation for us why The Guardians could snatch Alan Conway from under our noses on the day we were due to question him. We are all very interested in what you have to say."

"Well, Sir, I am as astonished as you at this turn of events. I have known Alan for several years, and not once have I ever had any cause to feel he was not a genuine believer that time travel is impossible. All his scientific papers have reinforced this view, and he has always strongly defended this. I can't think of any reason The Guardians would kidnap him."

"That may be the case," said the man impatiently, in a cloud of cigar smoke, "But what are you doing about finding him, and bringing him to Hive headquarters?"

"First, we are speaking to people at the convention who know Alan, to find if they know of his whereabouts. Second, I am arranging for various teams to contact all our sources of information in the city, to see if anyone has seen either Alan or a member of The Guardians tonight."

"Good, I'm glad to see you're taking positive action towards his return. Keep me updated hourly, this is your top priority, and failure will not be tolerated. Now get to work!"

"Yes sir," said Derek. He stood up and moved towards the door, which the butler had opened for him.

That could have been a lot worse, he thought while realising it would definitely get worse if he failed. *Now all I need to do is find Alan and get him back here.*

Chapter 6

Once inside, they showed Alan up a flight of stairs to a door that led to his quarters. It contained a large room, with an en-suite bathroom, toilet, shower and wash-hand basin, and a bedroom. He went into the bedroom, his luggage was waiting for him. The Guardians were very efficient, he thought. He unpacked and prepared for his first night in the room.

The next morning, he went downstairs for breakfast, where he met the other group members, and also, to his amazement, his old friend Karl Stepek.

"Karl, did they kidnap you as well?" he asked.

"Hello Alan, no, in fact, I am a member of the group, and I am delighted to see you. I am sure you will find this meeting of minds of great interest, and we also hope to learn things from you."

After breakfast, Karl took Alan to meet the leader of the group.

Karl knocked on a door. "Come in," said a voice and they both went through into a large bright room. There was a large table in the middle of the room, with two chairs on one side, and a single occupied chair on the other. The person seated was looking at some papers on the table.

"Take a seat," he said. "I'll be with you in a moment."

As they were waiting, Alan looked around the room and admired a painting of an angler with a magnificent salmon leaping in the distance. "Hello again, Alan," said the voice.

Alan looked over to the desk. "You!" he gasped.

Staring at him with a smile on his face was Mac, the cab driver from the airport. "It's good to see you, I hope you'll enjoy your stay with us, " Mac said.

He continued, "Now, I know you do not believe time travel is possible, and have written many papers proving this, which is one reason our competitors were so keen to sponsor you. And we hope to prove to you beyond a doubt that it is. If we can convince you, then we come to another reason you are here. We believe that once you understand our concepts, you can help us overcome a problem we cannot solve. Now I will leave you with Karl for now, and he will introduce you to the team who will answer any questions you have. You can also call on Tolka and me."

Returning to the larger room, Karl introduced him to the people he would work with over the next few weeks. "First, we have the engineer in our group, Mr David Tyrel, who will explain the workings of 'The Mirror,' and Ms Maria Sharkey and I, who will cover the mathematical concepts and equations involved. I think it would be better if David gave you some real-life examples to help you realise the reality of time travel."

David moved forward and shook Alan's hand. He was slim, with blond hair, of medium height, a ready smile, and a pleasant face. "I think the first thing to do is give you another taste of time travel. I believe your first encounter was a bit of a cheat, as no one had told you it was going to happen and it could be rather alarming.

"First, I will explain the mechanics at a simple level. We use what we call a 'Mirror' as our doorway to pass through time. There are controls on the 'Mirror' to allow us to set the date that we want to arrive at. So, for example, if you wanted to go back to yesterday evening, when you first arrived you would set the time to yesterday at 8:15 pm. Now we have here our 'Mirror' which I have already set, so you only need to step through it, then go to the top of the stairs, out of view of the front door, and watch yourself arrive. Once you have done this, come back to the 'Mirror' and step through to return here."

Alan looked at the three of them, gazing at him expectantly. "Well," he said half-jokingly, "I have always wanted to see what I look like from another person's viewpoint."

He walked towards the 'Mirror', hesitated a moment, then stepped through it, where he found himself at the top of the stairs, out of sight around the corner. He stood there waiting until he heard the doorbell ring and the murmur of voices. He quietly moved forward and looked down the stairs towards the door. There was Tolka, the driver, and himself coming into the entrance. Alan felt an icy shiver running down his spine as he stood looking at himself, but could not argue with the evidence of his own eyes. Time travel was possible. Quietly he slipped back to the 'Mirror' and walked through from the other side to find himself back beside Karl, David and Maria.

He stood looking at them for a moment. Astounded, he said, "It appears I've a lot to learn, but if you're willing to teach me, then let's get started."

Chapter 7

When Derek returned to the Eliot Hotel, he arranged for a team of Hive members to ask all the scientists who knew Alan Conway if they remembered seeing him at the Awards Ceremony. After they had done this, all the statements were returned to him.

Later in the afternoon, he examined them, looking for anything unusual. As time wore on, he became anxious, as there did not seem to be anything suspicious in any of the statements he had read. Just then, he picked up the statement from Karl Stepek, a loyal member of Hive, read through it and placed it in the rest of the pile. He was reaching for the next statement, when he paused, took up the previous statement and re-read it. Wait a minute, he thought. I saw Karl sitting next to Alan at the Awards Ceremony. How could he have forgotten to mention that in his statement, especially as they are such good friends?

He placed Karl's statement to the side and worked his way through the rest of them in case there were any others discrepancies.

He drove back to Hive Headquarters and immediately made inquiries about Karl's whereabouts.

"He was in his laboratory earlier today," said an assistant. "I'm not sure if he's still there."

As Derek was going to the lab, he saw Karl leave, but instead of calling out to him, he spoke to a member of his staff. "I want you to get a group of our men to follow Karl," he said. "Don't stop him, just follow him and note where he goes, then come back directly to me with a full update. Under no circumstances must you lose him at any point."

*

Later that evening the group leader reported back to him with details of Karl Stepek's travels for the day. This had included a visit to a supermarket, a trip to a coffee shop, where he met a group of people, and finally he returned to his flat.

"Very well," said Derek." I want your team to keep a watching brief on Karl for the next week. If he goes back to that coffee shop, I want your team to photograph who he meets, then follow them and see if they go back to a common location."

After the man left, Derek sat back in his chair and smiled. If I am right, he thought, this group of people could be members of The Guardians, and I could go to the directors with the location of their headquarters.

This could be my chance to get a giant promotion, maybe even a seat on The Board.

Chapter 8

For the first three weeks, Alan worked with David, learning how to use the 'Mirror'. He explained the technical details behind the settings so he could adjust the size of the frame as required. This meant the 'Mirror' could be as large or as small as necessary. It could shrink down to pocket-size if required and then enlarge it when needed.

Before Alan went on his first trip back in time, he had to have a meeting with Mac.

"Take a seat," said Mac as Alan entered the room. "Everyone who goes back in time must be aware there is one fundamental rule they must obey, without exception. Always remember that you are only a viewer in time and you should do nothing that could affect the timeline. Members of Hive and The Guardians all obey this rule as it could have catastrophic effects on humanity if broken.

"Let me explain to you why you are here, and how we hope you will assist us. As you know, 'Hive' is the corporation that sponsored the event you attended and indeed some of your own research. What you may now realise is that they have been trying to create the tech-nology to make time travel possible, and indeed have accomplished it. Despite that they continue to sponsor individuals like yourself to promote the opposite. This was to eliminate the possibility of another group start-ing up against them.

"We have the same technology. The fundamental difference between us is that we believe that time travel should gather knowledge and understanding, to correct and document any mistakes in historical records that have occurred. Hive wants to use this ability for their benefit. We have long held suspicions they were sending people back in time to perform certain acts, which, while not having a direct effect on humanity, would allow them to benefit in the future. An example of this would be manipulating the stock market. The knowledge of which companies are flourishing at present means they can send someone into the past to buy shares at a reduced price, and then come back and sell them for a considerable profit.

"Examples of this would be the computer industry, IBM, Digital and Apple, the manufacturers of digital age products, such as mobile phones, cameras, and watches. Using this approach certain Hive board members have become extremely wealthy without causing suspicion. Morally and ethically, we oppose them for what they are doing, but we cannot think of any way to stop this from happening. I suppose from their viewpoint, they have discovered the ultimate in insider dealing.

"So now you understand that we want to use time travel for humanity's benefit and how we differ from "Hive.""

Alan nodded his agreement and pondered the conundrum of how to stop the abuse of time travel.

*

The next day David told Alan that he would go with him on a trip to the 18th Century, to show him what life was like. As this would be his first trip, David would go with him as a guide and mentor.

David guided Alan to a room where he showed him several articles of clothing. "We need to wear these, so we fit in with our surroundings. Before we go, we need to leave all items of jewellery, watches, spectacles, mobile phones. Basically anything that would mark us as being out of the ordinary."

"How do you know what the people of that time would wear in such great detail?" asked Alan." After all, you can't exactly ask Google."

"There are some records but to be sure we use drones to do some reconnaissance work for us first."

He took Alan into a room that had several devices available for use. "When we are exploring a new time zone, we always send a drone through on several trips to let us know what to expect.

"Surely there's a risk in sending through something as technological advanced as drones."

"There is, but we have reduced it." He reached into a box and pulled out a drone no bigger than the palm of his hand.

"How can you possibly make them so small?. I was expecting something about a metre square." said Alan.

"Yes, our technical team is very skilled. The drone's clear perspex bodies make them virtually invisible. There are micro cameras, front, back, below and above, and proximity sensors that work on the same principle as those on your car when you are reversing towards a wall. This ensures that the drone will not collide with an object and damage itself. The drones are autonomous and programmed to travel vertically 30 metres, then perform a circle of 1500 metres, recording sound and vision, before they return through the 'Mirror'.

"If for any reason they do not return within 10 minutes of the expected time, we send a signal via the 'Mirror' to the drone, which will cause the gradual disintegration of the device. This ensures that no one from the past would ever receive a technical instrument from the future. Assuming they return, we then examine the recording taken and, using the information we have received, we decide on the next trip for the drone. It may take as many as a dozen drone trips before we have enough information for a traveller to go through the 'Mirror'.

"If you're ready, go into the fitting room and get yourself ready to fit in."

When Alan finally looked at himself in a mirror, he was wearing an outfit comprising a full-skirted knee-length coat, knee breeches, a long waistcoat (having sleeves), a linen shirt with frills and linen under-drawers.

He felt ridiculous, but David said he would fit in perfectly and would not receive a second glance. They both stepped through the mirror that was set for 1785. Everything around them changed, and Alan gasped in amazement to find himself in the middle of a forest.

Before they moved off to the village, David took a small whistle out of his pocket and blew into it. As Alan watched, the 'Mirror' vanished.

David explained that this disabled the functionality of the device until they returned so no one could accidentally walk through it while they were away." Whatever you do, don't lose the whistle," he said, and placed it carefully in his pocket.

They walked through a wooded area, and in the distance, Alan could hear sounds that gradually became louder until they were standing on the outskirts of a small town.

"Don't attract attention to yourself," whispered David. "We will look for a small tavern and I will book a room. This will be our base as we explore the area. It will also be where we eat our meals, so try to speak as little as possible, and be inconspicuous. Leave the talking to me."

As they walked through the town, Alan saw men and women wearing various hats and wigs, the men with frock coats and breeches, while the women wore bonnets and gowns of several layers.

"This looks a likely place to stay," said David. "We'll see if they have a room available."

Alan looked up to see a sign that said "The Crosse Keys." He pushed open the door, and they both entered. David went up to the landlord and asked for a room for himself and his friend, and a meal and a jug of ale while the room was being prepared.

They looked around and saw an empty table, so they sat down. Alan leaned forward and whispered, "I could hardly understand a word you said, I'm glad you told me to keep quiet for this trip."

"Language, like clothing changes through time. It's another thing we have to be aware of," David replied softly.

A serving girl arrived with their meal and left plates with bread and meat, an earthenware jug and two mugs. Alan looked for the cutlery, but there wasn't any. David passed him an extra knife from his pocket and said the tavern expected travellers to use their personal knives or daggers to cut the meat from the communal plate and place it on the bread to eat. They poured themselves a mug of ale from the jug. After his initial surprise at eating a slice of cold, greasy meat on a thick hunk of bread, he found he enjoyed it, and the ale had a sweet, fruity taste, which was quite pleasant.

After the meal, the landlord showed them to their room. It was furnished with two wooden benches and two rough mattresses filled with straw. The next morning they went down for breakfast to find that bacon, bread and eggs were being served with ale to drink, which they both enjoyed.

After the meal, they set out to explore the village. David suggested that if they saw any stalls selling food, they might buy something for their lunch. As they walked through the village Alan noticed several horse-drawn carts selling fruit and fish, so they purchased a loaf, cheese and some apples.

They walked around the village and watched some children playing. As they were looking for somewhere to have their lunch, they walked over a bridge and sat next to a tree. As they sat enjoying the food, Alan saw a young boy playing with his friends near the river. Suddenly he heard a splash and looked up to see the lad struggling in the water, with his friends standing by, looking helpless. Alan went to get up, but David grabbed his arm. "You can do nothing!" he said urgently. "You can't interfere with the timeline."

Alan watched in horror, while David held him. The boy's struggles became weaker until finally, he disappeared beneath the water.

"We could have saved him," whispered Alan."

"Yes," said David, sadly," We could, but we don't know what effect that would have had in the future."

"What effect could a boy in a small town possibly have?"

"That boy could have saved a general who was supposed to die and affect the course of a battle. The possibilities are too many and too awful to think about. It's why we have the rules."

Back in the tavern, they were both subdued. Alan still thought about the young boy, and David left him with his silent musings.

Once they were back in the room, David turned to Alan." Do you expect to go on several trips?. We are certainly interested in making use of your technical expertise, which is why Mac brought you to the group. However, we would expect everyone who joins our group to go on several trips to make them understand what we are trying to achieve."

"I'm not sure," Alan replied. This trip had proved more trying than he expected.

The following day they left the village in a different direction, and Alan saw more of the people and lifestyle of that era.

On the trip the next day they set off in another different direction. As they walked along, Alan noticed a patchwork of small fields and pointed this out to David.

"Yes," he said," They grow oats and barley, as well as root crops, such as turnip, onions, and beetroot in this region."

Later, as they were walking towards a farm, two horse-drawn wagons, laden with crops, passed them, heading towards the village.

"It must be the market day today. The centre of the village will be busy with people selling their produce," said David.

Soon they reached a farm with dairy cows in a field, and pigs, ducks and chickens in the yard.

"Life is certainly a lot different from our time," said Alan, "If we want to go out for a loaf, or a pound of sausages, we just go to the supermarket, but here you've got to make it yourself."

Alan found he was picking out some words by listening to the people, and although it was hard, he thought he was picking up fragments of their conversation. That night at the evening meal, Alan asked David how long this trip would last.

"Usually it is for seven days, although sometimes it might be longer. Why do you ask?."

" Well, to be honest, I'd kill to have a bath or a shower. How often do people here normally get washed?."

" Normally once or twice a year," smiled David, "I wondered when you would ask. All the mentors take bets when a new start goes into the field, of how long it will be before they miss their creature comforts. It will please you to know that you now hold the record time of four days, by the time we return tomorrow. And then it's a fight to see who reaches the showers first."

The following morning it was time to go back to their own time. They walked out of the village towards where the mirror should have been, but Alan could see nothing. He was getting concerned when David reached into his pocket and pulled out the small whistle. As he blew into it, the mirror appeared, and they both walked through it and back into the house.

"Well done Alan, now off you go for your well-earned shower, then rest and have a meal. Mac will want to see you later for a debrief."

Over the next few weeks, Alan travelled to different times with David as a guide, showing him what life was like for different centuries. He gained knowledge of how people lived during the 10th, 14th and 18th Centuries, the struggles they had to survive, and also the closeness they displayed for the family group. These were only brief visits, however, to give him a glimpse of what life was like in those times, and the greatest differences he noticed were the clothes the people wore, the food they ate, and even the language they spoke, which was difficult to understand.

After completing his initiation on the practical side of the project, and working out on the field, David said that he felt Alan had a good understanding of how to use the "Mirror" and that he could now transfer to Karl Stepek and Maria Sharkey for the next part of his training, which covered the theory and mathematics of time travel.

Chapter 9

The next day, after breakfast, Alan met Karl.

"Good morning," Karl smiled. "How did you enjoy the time you spent with David experiencing life in the different centuries?."

"It was fascinating and very educational, now I am eager to find out what you have to teach me."

Over the next weeks in the group, Alan became familiar with the theory behind time travel, and Karl or Maria quickly answered any questions raised.

They explained how, when attempting to achieve time travel, they initially tried to discover how to monitor the space/timeline, as this would allow them to define a time that they wanted to visit. After many setbacks and dead ends, they discovered that the method used to achieve this was by monitoring the properties of quarks on the path that was taken by the drone as it passed through the "Mirror." They discovered the results returned from the drone proved the value of the quarks monitored was always a positive, or "UP" quark.

"Was this because of detecting the various quarks?" asked Alan

"No," said Karl, "Initially they tried several various particles, such as leptons. Atoms, electrons and neutrons, until finally, they tried quarks. Luckily, the first one they tried was the "UP" quark and found success.

Using this approach, they could now travel back in time and return to the current time.

*

One day, as Alan was working with Maria on enhancements to the time monitor to improve the fine detail necessary to increase the accuracy of the dates arrived at, Karl came over and sat with them.

"Has Maria mentioned to you about a problem that we call 'The Wall'?"

Alan shook his head.

"It occurs when we try to go forward into the future, and until now, no one in our group, and also Hive, can overcome it. We can travel back in time, but not in the future. If we try to do this, the 'Mirror' will prevent anything from passing through it.

"This is another reason we wanted you to join us. We feel that a fresh mind, without blinkers, might see a way to overcome this issue. From now on, we would like you to work on this problem. You can work without distractions, and with all the resources you need. We will assist you in any way we can."

From that day on, Alan dedicated his time looking at the theory and practice behind 'The Mirror.'

His investigations into the mechanism of time led him to believe that current time only lasted for a small fraction of a second before it became past time. This would mean that future-time would also have a value in the instant before it became current time and then past-time.

One night as he was working alone, making his modifications to the control mechanism, he tried a simple test to prove that his theory worked.

In his experiments with the mechanism in 'The Mirror', he tested them with every value for the various quarks; "UP," "DOWN," "TOP," "BOTTOM," "CHARM," and "STRANGE."

After several failures, he used the negative or "DOWN" quark, to see if this would allow an object to pass through 'The Mirror' into the future.

He set the time to 5 seconds in 'The Mirror' and threw a pillow into it, then waited to see what would happen…

The pillow vanished, then appeared through 'The Mirror' five seconds later.

Alan had done it. He had overcome the barrier, and time travel into the future was now a possibility, it was a matter of experimenting further to see how far into the future the device would allow them to travel.

His next test involved using a drone. He set the time in 'The Mirror' to 15 minutes and programmed the drone to go through it, then up 5 metres, then travel through a circular tour of 5 metres, before returning.

The drone travelled through 'The Mirror' and returned 5 minutes later. Alan took the recording of the trip and played it back on his computer. As he expected, the journey showed the inside of the room he was working in.

As the drone started moving round in its circular route, Alan saw himself appear on the screen, although he knew he had not seen the drone appear above him during its journey. Alan now had definite proof that it was possible to go into the future. First, he reset 'The Mirror' to its standard values so only he would know the settings, as he realised the enormous implications his discovery could mean for humanity.

He decided this was something that the others needed to see, so he went to visit Mac and asked if he could provide an update to the group on his progress to date.

"Certainly," said Mac, "we'd all be very interested to see how you are getting on. Would 3 p.m. tomorrow suit?"

Alan agreed and went back to the room, where he placed seating for the people who would arrive for his update the following day. He borrowed a drone, then went to 'The Mirror,' which he had adapted. He adjusted the time to 24 hours into the future and programmed the drone to go forward, then go up 5 metres, then travel through a circular tour of 5 metres, before returning. When the drone returned, Alan took the recording of the trip and played it back on his computer. As expected, he saw various people arriving and taking their seats before the update. Then he borrowed a screen on which he could display the output from his computer on the wall at the end of the hall, so everyone could see it.

The next day, it was nearly 3 o'clock, and the hall had almost every seat taken.

Mac came to the front, next to Alan, and said, "Now you all know that Alan has been investigating the problem we have been having with 'The Mirror,' where it blocks every attempt we have made to go into the Future. He is going to update us on how his work has been progressing so far."

Mac sat down, and everyone turned to look at Alan. Nervous, Alan took a deep breath, and said, "Before I start, I would like to show you all a recording I took when I sent a drone through 'The Mirror' yesterday."

He started the recording. The image showed the drone as it rose almost to the ceiling of the room, then began moving around. Soon you could view the rows of chairs, with people moving into the various seats until it was almost full. By now the drone was dropping and moving towards 'The Mirror,' then the recording stopped. Alan stood and faced the group," What you saw was a recording I made yesterday when I sent the drone through 'The Mirror' with the time set for today at 2:45 pm," he said.

There was total silence as the people in the hall suddenly grasped what they had seen, then they erupted!.

Everyone was jumping up and down, hugging each other and giving high fives, screaming, weeping tears of joy, kissing each other. They all realised that they had seen history being made. Alan had achieved the impossible, and at that point he almost disappeared under a wave of exultant men and women, all wanting to congratulate him.

It took a while before Mac could extricate him from the tangled mass of people, but once things had calmed down, he took him aside.

"Alan, that was the most restrained statement of a historical achievement I have ever seen; a classic example of the British understatement at its very best, " Mac said with a broad grin.

Alan looked at him and said, "You realise we are going to have to do some very hard thinking about how we can use this new ability. It could be more dangerous than travelling back through time."

"I agree," he said." We will need to get a team to look at the rules we will need to put in place covering almost every scenario for the use of travelling into the Future. We will celebrate tonight and then we need to send the drones to gather information for us, so that we know what those dangers might be."

Chapter 10

After several discussions, the team felt that if they sent drones through 150 and then 300 years into the future, they could then make comparisons and judgments about what they were doing.

When the drones returned, the group studied the information each drone had brought back.

They felt that the changes in 150 years were fairly minor in areas such as architecture, travel and behaviour of the population. There did not seem to be radical changes or improvements which would provide major benefits to the current time.

The results from the second drone, 300 years in the future, were more marked in the population's behaviour, and the group felt this would require further investigation before they could send in a team of visitors.

Over the next three weeks, they extended the drones' search area and length of stay to allow them to collect more data. On their return, they watched the results and discussed their thoughts on what they had seen.

"I'm concerned with the lack of emotion that the population are showing," said Alan, "They all seem to walk around like a bunch of zombies, there are hardly any signs of laughter, humour, anger, nor empathy from the people we have seen. They just seem to walk through the day without a purpose. I also didn't notice any open cafes or shops, for people to visit."

"I agree," said Mac," We will need to send in two teams to get some feedback."

They decided that Alan and David should be in one team, and Maria and Karl in the other.

Alan and David went through 'The Mirror' first and found themselves in a narrow lane.

"That was fortunate," said Alan. "Can you imagine if we had come out in the middle of a road?."

They both walked along to the end of the lane and turned into a major street. All the transport was silent, which seemed to show they were using an electric car, or some other form of power, and also the passengers were facing in the opposite direction to where the car or bus was travelling. Another puzzling aspect was they could not see who the driver was.

Alan noticed a car further down the street. "Look, there is a parked car, let's see what the layout of the controls looks like ." As they both slowly walked by the car, he noticed that there was no dashboard, gearstick, handbrake and most surprising of all, no steering wheel." As they were walking past, David said to him," There's a shop window, let's stand at it and pretend to look at the display, while we discuss what we've seen so far."

"What immediately strikes me," said Alan," is the almost total lack of noise. We are both standing at the side of a busy road, and there's hardly a sound, it's eerie."

Just then, a family with two young children walked up to the parked car. They all entered the vehicle, then they both noticed the man speaking, and the car immediately drove off smoothly into the flow of traffic.

"Was the car voice-activated?" asked David." I didn't see him start the car or control it, it just seemed to respond to his voice. Perhaps they've gone fully autonomous now for all vehicles, although what system could control this level of traffic volume I do not know. It must be incredibly powerful."

Meanwhile, Maria and Karl were entering a park where they saw a group of people. They both sat down on a park bench, where they could observe them without being noticed, and quietly discuss their findings.

"I am finding it very odd that they are all walking around the pond in the centre of the park in the same direction, at about the same speed. You would expect people to walk all over the place in different directions," said Maria."Another thing, where are all the pets?. You usually see people out walking their dogs, young children running about playing, or mothers walking with their babies in prams or buggies, but I don't see that either. It almost reminds me of those old films where you see the convicts taking their exercise break in the prison, all walking around in a circle. And can you hear any sounds of wildlife, ducks or swans in the pond for example?"

"You're right, although there are people out here, there are no joggers, cyclists, kids on skateboards, or whatever the equivalent would be in this era. Perhaps they are doing it all at a home gymnasium where they can exercise in a virtual world. We would need to get into someone's house to see what the furniture of the future looks like."

As they both stood up to walk away, he said, "I've just noticed something. Look at the grass in the park. Can you see any litter? and it doesn't look like normal grass, it's artificial, it's so even and clipped. Even the leaves in the trees look green, even though it's Autumn."

"Do you see any fallen leaves?. Everything is just too perfect, it's not natural."

Suddenly Maria gripped his arm, "Look at all the people, why are they staring at us?."

"Let's get back to 'The Mirror,' said Karl urgently," I think people have noticed us talking to each other, and I've got a bad feeling about this."

As they walked toward the exit of the park, they saw all the people moving to stop them from leaving.

"Run!," said Karl. They both raced out of the park, down the street, then turned into the lane where Karl pulled out the whistle and blew into it. As 'The Mirror' appeared, Maria ran through it, but as Karl was about to go after her, he turned to look back. It shocked him to see a howling mob racing towards him, so he quickly stepped into 'The Mirror' and returned to the safety of his own time.

Chapter 11

The next meeting of the group was a solemn affair after Alan and David had reported on their findings, followed by the disturbing news from Karl and Maria.

Everyone in the group agreed that something had happened between them in the one-hundred and fifty years between journeys to cause this radical change in the population, but what could it have been?

Alan went to Mac and suggested that if the group had no objections, he would investigate this in smaller time increments, and when he had something to report, he would come back with his findings.

Everyone agreed with this, and so Alan was once more left alone to carry on with his project, and they agreed he would use five-yearly increments to home in on when the change had occurred.

Over the next three weeks, Alan sent the drones through 'The Mirror' covering different years in unique patterns and durations to see if he could identify what might have caused the changes.

It was in the 285th year into the future, early in the morning, when Alan was viewing the drones' video, that he saw a strange glittering cloud that covered the entire land. Alan knew that the drone was travelling at a height of 100 metres and he could see nothing in the video except this mist. He sent a drone to the 281st year and viewed the results.

Based on the drones' recorded findings, everything was normal from the viewpoint of the behaviour of the population. The results were the same for the 282nd year, however, on the 283rd year, the video showed the mist, but it seemed far higher, as the cloud was darker. Alan sent a second drone through but programmed it to start it at a height of 300 metres.

Through the use of progressive drones, Alan could finally work out what had happened.

Based on his findings, he went to see Mac.

"Mac," he said," I'd like to show you the results, so we can decide what to do next."

"Certainly," said Mac, "Let me see what you've found."

"I needed to find when the change first occurred, so I moved from year 280. Everything seemed okay, so I moved forward a year at a time, and everything stayed the same until year 283."

As Mac watched the recording, he gave a sharp exclamation, "What's that strange mist in the air?"

"I'm not sure, but it is covering everything, and in year 285 I sent the drone up 350 metres before it broke out above the mist."

"How did they spray this mist, was it a plane, a rocket, how could it have achieved this level of coverage?

"I don't know, but the spray seems to have been heavier than air. Through time, you gradually saw trees, buildings, and eventually, towns and villages as the gas sank toward ground level.

It's the next recording that is the most alarming though," said Alan.

They both watched as drones flew through the towns and villages, telling everyone to go to the nearest school for the population to be tagged, then receive Safety Training.

As they watched people going into a school, they saw a uniformed man wearing a mask walking up and down a row of people, keeping them in line.

"Who's he?" said Mac

"Look at the badge on his arm."

He zoomed in on the image to get a closer look.

Mac cried with horror, "That's the Hive badge."

"Yes," they must have decided that just being wealthy was not enough. They wanted to have power as well, and the ultimate level of power would be world domination.

"Now, however, we are aware of their plan, so if we go forward in time to when the idea first appeared and cause it to be cancelled, then the world would have a normal progression into the future without the certainty of "Hive" domination."

Mac's face was ashen as the enormity of Alan's findings sunk in.

"What should we do Mac?" asked Alan.

Mac stood and walked to the end of the office and looked out of the window for a long time.

We can't have a group meeting about this. I would say we should restrict it to Karl, David, Maria, you and me. I will arrange for a meeting at three."

When the meeting convened everyone was there except Karl and Alan.

I wonder where Alan's got to? There's no way he'd be late for this meeting," thought Mac.

Just then Karl walked into the room." Sorry I'm late," he said, "Alan asked me to give you this," and handed Mac a letter. Mac took it, sat down at his desk, and unfolded it.

Mac,

I knew this would happen when I came to see you this morning.

I said the information had to stay between the two of us, but I realise you cannot break the fundamental rule, and could not make any other decision, which will doom humanity to the tyranny of "Hive."

I feel that the only option is to go forward in time to when the scheme was first being dreamt up and ensure it never sees the light of day.

I have taken two "Mirrors, and three drones, and will send you my findings from time to time, to keep you up to date.

If I'm successful in preventing this "Hive" scheme from starting, I will return to re-join the group, if you'll have me.

I hope you will wish me well.

Alan.

THE PURPLE SHARD

Margaret Duffy

Chapter 1

CONVICTED OF MURDER ...CLAIMS WRONGLY CONVICTED... BUSINESSMAN WORTH £20 MILLION OFFERS HALF HIS WEALTH TO ANYONE WHO CAN PROVE HIS INNOCENCE.

£10 million! Really!

I froze, toast halfway to my mouth, gripping the newspaper so tightly it wrinkled. Toast back on the plate, I brushed off the crumbs and smoothed the paper.

Mind agape, I pored over the details that had been regurgitated from previous articles, drinking them in. Thierry Nicoll, aged 35, was found standing over the body of his best friend, Hamish Todd, holding a bloody shard of purple glass from an expensive vase; a Daum, French, part of his prized collection.

Earlier in the evening, they argued in their golf club-house and it turned physical. The barman separated them and said they reconciled before they left. They then went back to Nicoll's house. Nicoll claimed he passed out or was knocked out, and woke up to find his friend lying in a pool of blood with the shard sticking out of his chest. He pulled it out claiming he had some confused idea it would save him. Blood tests showed both with extremely high levels of alcohol. The police seemed to regard it as an open and shut case; the jury agreed and found him guilty.

I would give anything to get my hands on that reward.

*

Livy's voice penetrated. 'MUM! HELLO! Are you receiving me? I need to go...work calls.' She leaned over me kissing the top of my head. 'Are you okay? Your mouth's open like a fish.'

I snapped it closed. 'I'm fine, fine.' Feeling my face stiffen with a forced smile.

Livy walked to the other side of the table to her son, Peter. His headphones on, engrossed in his Nintendo Switch game, she knelt beside him. 'Peter,' she said gently.

No response.

'I'm going to work now Peter,' close to his ear, knowing what a sudden touch would do. 'You be good for Nana, OK?'

A slight turn of the head was the only indication that he had heard.

I watched them, burning love welling up in me for the silent boy. Sighing, she stood up, eyes bleak with that haunted, oh so familiar look. After she left, I sat watching Peter, brain whirling, visualising the possibilities for my plan and how that money could transform it into reality.

*

It was a big surprise when I received the Visit Order from Barlinnie Prison, commonly known in Glasgow as the Bar-L. It said that Thierry Nicoll had agreed to see me. On the agreed date, I arrived early, my head spinning with information and half-formed ideas; ignoring the smidgen of sense in the recess of my mind whispering it was a mad idea, another hare-brained scheme.

The outside of the prison was surprisingly welcoming, with its modern façade, not the Dickensian horror of my imagination. Still, I could feel my heart thumping and my tongue seemed to be stuck to the roof of my mouth as I waited to be called to the visitors' room.

'Nolly Towers!' A harsh voice summoned, and I went through for the rubdown search, legs a bit shaky. The female officer looked sympathetic. 'First time?'

I nodded.

'You'll get used to it.'

The table number was called. I needed to get a grip, look like I knew what I was doing.

Thierry Nicoll was handsome, his looks showing traces of his French and Algerian heritage. His tawny eyes widened, and he stared disbelievingly at me when I stopped at one of the seats opposite him.

'You are Nolly Towers?'

Gulping, trying to get some saliva going, I sat.

'I thought ... that you were a man! And ...' he paused inhaling sharply, 'that you would be younger.'

That stung. 'I'm fit and not that old.'

'You must be ... you look, well ... middle-aged ... and you have a limp.'

I am fifty-five but have been told I look younger, and I resented the implication. 'So what? Does having a limp stop my brain from working?'

That raised a slight smile. 'Well, you certainly don't lack nerve.' If only he knew. 'What makes you think you can prove me innocent?'

The tone was mild, and he looked curious, rather than aggressive but I was on my mettle, determined to prove myself.

'Do you think a woman can't do it?'

He shrugged.

'Why are you offering half your wealth? Who are you looking for? A magician?'

'No! I hoped that some super cool, amazing PI would pop up with brilliant ideas, not a middle-aged, grumpy woman.'

'Touché!' I grinned at him, and he returned it, those striking eyes warm. 'Look, I promise you I don't quit on anything I take on. Plus, I have a burning reason for wanting that money.'

The smile disappeared and he gave a 'hmph!' with a half-shake of his head.

'Listen, I'm being straight with you! And remember you asked me to come. So, make up your mind to give me a chance or I'm leaving.'

A sort of gasping laugh greeted this. 'You remind me of my mother. I still miss her.' His gaze turned inwards.

The murmurs of the other visitors and the odd clang of the snack machine, unnoticed until now, grew louder in the silence between us. I offered up a silent prayer, fear flooding me. I would never get another chance to realise my dream for Peter and other autistic children. This money would guarantee it.

'She was a determined woman and she made me what I am.' With another 'hmph,' this time sounding amused, he focused on me, a wide smile lighting up his face, displaying his perfect teeth. 'Are you always this bolshie?'

'More, or less,' I admitted. 'But I do have ideas...and I am determined.'

'Oh, that I could believe. Okay, what do you have in mind?'

'I think there were some gaps in the witness statements that were gathered for the Procurator Fiscal's Report.'

'So, you said in your letter. What gaps? And how do you know?'

'No...no freebies. First, you must agree to take me on.' Shaking my head and trying to look mysterious and sound confident, hiding the uncertainty of what was mainly guesswork from gossip acquired from a couple of sources. 'And I want it in writing.'

Another long pause, the smile slowly leaving his face and his eyes becoming thoughtful. The sounds of visitors taking leave grew louder and panic again tied my stomach in knots.

'Okay!' You're on!' he said, the smile returning. I had to fight an overwhelming urge to kiss him, settling instead for shaking his hand vigorously, more than a little convinced me reminding him of his mother swung it for me.

*

Rob Cheney, my next-door neighbour, usually came in on Wednesdays after Peter was dropped off from school. He was one of the few people Peter was comfortable with. As usual, I found them in the small, old conservatory at the back of the house. The sun was already low and cast a warm light on them, bending over a motherboard from a computer which was, as usual, in bits. Peter was fascinated with what made them work and Rob, a retired engineer, loved helping him. Apart from a quizzical glance at me he only said, 'Okay?'

'No problem.'

I made myself a cup of tea and stood staring out of the window at the White Cart, a tributary of the river Clyde, which ran along the back of the garden. A couple, arms around each other, were standing on the Snuff Mill Bridge gazing down at the water. Spring should have been well advanced as it was almost May, but cold, uncertain weather had had an effect and most of the daffodils in the garden had their yellow coats still tightly closed as though shivering in the chill breeze. I could feel Rob's eyes on me, so I moved to my writing table, opening the laptop and shuffling notes, but my attention kept drifting. When he had to leave saying he expected a call from his son I breathed a sigh of relief.

Later, after Livy collected Peter, Rob tapped lightly at the conservatory door.

I let him in. 'Coffee?'

'No thanks. Nolly!' stopping me as I made a move towards the kitchen. 'Wait a minute.'

'I want a coffee.'

'Please sit down. We need to talk.'

I stayed by the door. 'I know what I'm doing Rob.'

'I take it he agreed to hire you, then?' I nodded and walked back into the room sitting opposite him with a sigh, knowing what was coming.

Rob was a civil engineer, and he owned the other half of our semi-detached, Victorian house. He travelled the world, so I hardly knew him until his wife, Doris, contracted cancer: he took early retirement to stay at home, nursing her until she died. He said working with Peter helped him to cope, and Peter loved him. Gradually, I had come to depend on him a lot. I suppose we all had.

'Nolly, doing witness statements for the Procurator Fiscal's Office, and writing detective stories does not make you a private detective.'

'I'm not stupid, Rob, I know that. But what have I got to lose?'

He looked worried. 'You're always so gung-ho about everything and I think this could be dangerous ... in ways we can't even imagine.'

'Oh, for god's sake ... forget the coffee, let's have a drink, relax.'

Chapter 2.

Blanche Nicoll had all the hallmarks of wealth with her beautifully cut blonde hair, designer lounging outfit and immaculate fingernails. She towered over me, her grey eyes narrowed, and eyebrows raised. Expecting a maid, I was surprised when she opened the door of the Nicoll mansion in Newlands, a well-to-do suburb on the south side of the city. It was a blonde sandstone house with immaculate gardens and a huge conservatory built onto the side.

'Nolly Towers.' Holding out my hand, wide smile in place. 'Thank you for agreeing to see me.'

Grudgingly, she offered a couple of brilliant, red-tipped fingers, barely touching mine, then used them to signal for me to follow and led me through a large hall and lounge to the conservatory. The house had been completely and tastefully modernised, with pastel walls and lots of off-white leather sofas, designer coffee tables and expensive ornaments. I noted Daum vases and sculptures scattered around. Many of the original features such as fireplaces had been retained.

'Sit.' Another wave of the carmine gloss fingertips. 'Would you like a drink?'

'Yes, please. Anything soft.'

Crossing to the back wall she opened a concealed fridge in one of the units, taking out a bottle of real lemonade with a posh label. Every move she made looked rehearsed or as if she were on a show. Careful, languid movements carried out as she brought the bottle and a crystal glass over to me then placed them on a glass-topped occasional table at my elbow. She poured herself a Perrier and sat down opposite, a good ten feet away.

'Ms Towers, did you say?' I nodded, still smiling. 'Anything I can do to help; I will of course be very willing to do.'

'Thank you, I appreciate that.' Placing my phone on the side table I pressed record. 'Okay if I record this, Mrs Nicoll?'

She jumped like a scalded cat. 'NO!'

Quickly, I switched it off and waited, but she sat back, picked up her water and carefully sipped, watching me over the rim of the glass. A cat-like image popped into my head.

'Okay...would you mind going over for me what happened on the night of the murder?'

Speaking in a monotone she told how she had been out with friends and came home to find Thierry standing over the body of his friend holding a bloody shard of glass in his hand. A touch of relish crept into her voice as she described the bloody scene making me shiver.

'Forgive me for asking a personal question, but were you happily married, Mrs Nicoll?'

Her voice rose an octave. 'Of course! Why do you ask?'

'I just wondered.' A sinew in her neck stood out and her knuckles were white on the glass she clutched. Tense. Why? The little voice said do not go there, but I ignored it.

'Do you believe your husband is guilty?' She twitched, lips so tight the carmine lipstick disappeared, and her eyes bored into me even across the space.

'He was found guilty, wasn't he?'

'Of course, but forgive me...that's not really what I'm asking.'

Carefully, she picked up the Perrier and added some to her glass, but her hand shook a little, spilling some onto the glass table. She stared at the drops then swallowed and looked across at me.

'I don't know!'

'Do you think he is capable of murder? Was he violent towards you?'

'No! Why are you asking these questions? They are irrelevant. Shouldn't you be out trying to find whatever proof he thinks is out there?'

Despite the defiant tone, she looked uneasy, a lot less confident. I changed tack to keep here on my side, and cooperative.

'Your house is beautiful, I love it. Have you always lived here?' Indicating the décor.

A pause as she considered. 'It was originally Thierry's parents' home. When his father died Thierry moved in with his mother. After we married, he wanted to continue to live here.'

'You got on well with his mother?'

'What? What have you heard?' Another rise in volume with a muted touch of screech.

'Nothing...nothing. I'm just trying to get a picture of your lives.'

'I would think all you need are the facts related to the fight Thierry had with Hamish that night. What does my relationship with his mother have to do with the murder?'

She repeated what I already knew; that Thierry and Hamish had been drinking at the golf club all evening and had a violent row which the club barman broke up. They resolved their differences and left together.

'Why do you think they came back here?' I asked.

'How should I know? Probably wanted more drink. You know what men are like when they get to that stage of drunkenness, they only want more.'

'And was Thierry often violent when he got drunk?'

Her eyes narrowed considering. 'Well, he had a quick temper...and he is a jealous kind of man.'

'Jealous of Hamish? Or you?'

'Oh, it was crazy. He thought I was having an affair, a fling he called it, with Hamish. As if.' The contemptuous tone sounded real, but I wondered if she had given Thierry cause for jealousy. She struck me as the kind of woman who would bask in driving men mad. It surprised me that she gave the information so easily, but she probably thought Thierry would have told me.

'Well, if that is all, Ms Towers,' she stood up. 'I have an appointment soon.'

I was being dismissed. 'Would you mind if I have a proper look at the Daum collection?' I asked, with, hopefully, a winning smile.

With ill grace she took me into the large sitting room we had passed through. Carefully, she walked around the rug in the middle of the floor rather than going directly to the cabinet. Guessing that it covered a stain, relic of the bloody murder, I walked around it too.

The collection was breathtaking with a varied collection of centrepieces, bowls, and sculptures. It was set in specially lit cabinets in the wall on both sides of the white marble fireplace. A magnificent peacock stood alone on the top shelf and an empty space at the bottom, I suspected, was the place where the murder weapon had been. I tried to connect with Blanche by commenting on the beauty of an Art Deco figure of a ballerina, but she knew nothing about it and became increasingly edgy and impatient.

'Do you find it difficult to live in the house now?'

'No, why should I?'

'Well, it was originally your husband's parents' house. Does that bother you?'

'No!'

'Forgive me for asking, does it belong solely to your husband?'

'Yes, he bought that sister of his out.'

'Oh yes, Lailah, isn't it?'

'Lailah Kennedy. Calls herself Lil.'

'She runs the family business with your husband, doesn't she? How is she managing without him?'

'Knowing her she'll be in her element.'

She walked out into the hall and almost hustled me out, not exactly slamming the door but coming close. I sauntered down the drive then ducked into the bushes near the gate. Like a thief, I crept back towards the house so intent on keeping an eye on the French windows that I almost tripped over a man bending over a rose bed. He looked up at me in surprise.

'I ... I thought I dropped an ... n... earring,'

He squinted, eyes switching from me to the house and back. 'You visit Mrs Nicoll, I see you.' pointing his secateurs towards the windows. 'You not come out here. No earring!'

'Sorry ... sorry.' I smiled at him, scrunching my face into an apology. 'No, I didn't come out here, but I wanted to see the garden, and I think Mrs Nicoll has had enough of me snooping.'

That caused a furrow in his forehead as he considered this. 'Snooping? What is this?'

'Asking questions.'

'Ah! Okay!' He stood up, brushing the dirt from his hands onto his frayed jeans. He sounded Eastern European.

'Polish?' I asked.

'Romany. Mrs Nicoll, you are friend?'

'No, I am a private investigator. Mister Nicoll employed me to find out who is the real killer of his friend.'

He considered this for a long time, nodding and pursing his lips, brown eyes never leaving my face. 'Mister Nicoll is a good man. The Mrs is not so good,' shaking his head for emphasis. 'Bad temper, bad.'

The French windows crashed open, and Blanche called out shrilly, 'Get on with your work, I don't pay you to gossip.' He bent over the rose bush and refused to say any more.

*

As I walked into my house my mobile rang. It was the estate agent for the property.

'Ms Towers, I'm sorry to bother you but I would like to confirm that you are going ahead with your offer.'

'Yes, of course.'

'Good, good. Ehm! We can expect the deposit to secure it, soon, then?'

'Oh, of course.'

*

Liv arrived soon after with Peter who rushed out to the trampoline. We watched him from the window, coffee mugs in hand.

'Livy, can I ask you for a huge favour?'

'Of course, Mum...anything.'

'You're in a good mood! Good day?'

'Yeah, Peter's teacher is pleased with him. Says he's making great progress with his writing.'

Peter's writing was usually cramped and small, squeezed into a corner of the page and hard to read. His teacher was trying out a new aid.

'That's great love.'

'So, what's the favour, Ma?'

'Well, I need info about the Nicoll case...and I thought...'

'What?'

'That may be that detective sergeant you know...eh-...Steele, is it? Maybe he would give me some intel on the case.'

'Seriously, Mum!' That could cost him his job. Anyway, I don't know him that well.'

'Well enough to make you blush when you mention him. Fancies you, does he?'

'Mum, are you saying — even if it's true — that I should use that to get info?'

'No, well not really, but it would help me so much. Please, it's for Peter.'

I felt a twinge of shame but I pushed it away. 'He was on the team that investigated, wasn't he?'

'Well, he was promoted to it about halfway through.'

My darling daughter looked out at Peter jumping happily on the trampoline — one of the most successful ways to keep him happy and relaxed — and her expression softened.

In for a penny, I pushed harder. 'I've already asked around my connections through the precognition crowd who work for the procurator but no joy so far. I'm stuck, Livy. I need more info on the case.'

'Mum, I don't know why you are so hell-bent on this anyway. You don't need the money.' A thought struck her, and she stared at me. 'What do you mean it's for Peter?'

'Oh, sorry Liv, that was to put pressure on you. I didn't mean anything.' I could not tell her my plan; she would go ballistic. She already thought I launched myself into projects without any regard for the consequences.

'This could be dangerous!' she continued, putting her arm around my shoulder. 'He's been found guilty. If he's innocent, it means that someone out there did it. And thinks he or she is safe!'

I hugged her tightly. 'I know, Liv, honestly I do. But I've committed myself now and you know how important keeping my word is to me.'

She sighed, squeezing my shoulder. 'Oh, Ma, you're a nightmare but I'll see what I can do.'

The sudden crack of a firework exploded nearby, and Peter started screaming. We both ran out. He must have forgotten to put on his ear defenders and was rolling about, hands covering his ears. Livy unzipped the cover of the trampoline and climbed in. She tried to calm him but just then another loud bang rang out. Peter writhed around. Livy tried to get him out and into the house. She managed to get him to the edge, but he gave a sudden twist and rolled out. He stood up, and lunged at the flowerpots, lifting a pot of geraniums, smashing it down on another one. He rampaged around the garden, screaming, and lashing out at anything in his way, Livy running desperately behind him, trying to calm him and stop him from hurting himself again as in previous meltdowns. It was the worst incident in months but, sadly, still quite frequent. My daughter caught blows to her face and body as she tried to calm Peter. Blood was streaming from her forehead where a flying fragment hit it.

We were both wiped out by the time she finally got him inside and focused on a favourite TV show.

*

Rob breezed in later. I was slumped on the couch, staring out at the garden, still shaken.

'Stuck on the last clue but finally got a corker. Pleased with it.'

He never missed a deadline on his weekly crossword submission to the local paper. In the past, I had attempted a couple but ended up with a headache. 'And what have you got up to in the last couple of days?' Noticing my silence, he crossed the room and sat down close to me. 'Oh no! A meltdown?'

Unusually, he put his arm around me and gently stroked my forehead. Tears welled up and I leaned into him, sobbing uncontrollably.

'Every time we think we have a good handle on what to do, something happens. It's exhausting, Rob, but more debilitating for Livy. She never gets a rest.'

'Shhh! You're both wonderful and it's amazing how well you've coped.'

I swallowed and tried to straighten up, but he held onto me with a firm touch. His hand was comforting, and I became aware of his warm breath in my ear. Gently he turned my face towards him. The kiss marked a change in our so-far platonic, if deep, friendship. I lost myself in the touch of his lips, his body moving closer, realisation that we had been moving towards this dawning on me. His smell was familiar and comforting.

'NO!' I jumped up, backing away as though scalded. 'I'm sorry Rob, I can't do this!'

The look on his face was comical. One minute I was as full-on as he was, now my arms were windmilling around my head like a maniac.

'Okay, Nolly, it's fine,' he said, soothingly but his face was white, and he looked wounded.

'There's just so much on my mind, Rob,' I stammered. 'You're a great comfort to all of us. But...but it might be better for things to stay the way they were.'

'Okay, maybe you're right.' He got up, walked to the window, looking out into the darkness. I could find nothing to say but I felt relieved. A sexual relationship with all its implications of intimacy would be too much to cope with on top of everything else, even if my body was craving it.

When he eventually turned around, he was smiling, the same old Rob, looking so handsome with laughter lines crinkling around his blue eyes and creasing his face. What was wrong with me, pushing away something I longed for? I gave myself a shake. It would have to wait.

'Okay Nolly, I know you haven't told me all that's going on with this centre you're so passionate about. What gives?'

With a smile, I waved him towards the old leather chair, his usual seat. With a rueful smile and a shrug, he sat. As I told him about my vision for the centre; the outdoor activities and horse riding as well as intensive teaching on computer skills according to the children's abilities; adrenaline surged through me.

Finally, I ran out of breath, Rob had been completely silent, but his eyes held a look I recognised. I coughed glad we were not sharing the sofa. With that look, I wouldn't have been able to control myself. 'Sorry, got a bit carried away.'

'It's amazing, Nolly, an inspired project.'

I had left out how far I had already committed myself to a property in Ayrshire with extensive grounds which needed massive investment.

'What about Nicoll? Any theories? And most importantly do you think he did it?'

'I don't think so.'

'How so?'

'He loves his Daum collection...it's amazing, Rob. I don't think he would use a rare vase as a weapon, no matter how provoked or drunk he was.'

'Mmm! People do strange things when driven by rage…it's possible.'

'It just doesn't fit. Hamish was killed by a shard, which means the vase was already broken.'

'Could have been dropped accidentally. That would have enraged Nicoll.'

'Maybe the victim was meant to be Thierry. I believe that he was knocked out, as he claims.'

'And? Why wasn't he killed?'

I shrugged helplessly, 'I don't know. Blanche came in, or she was there all the time. Maybe the real killer fled. Maybe she let him out?'

'Doesn't make sense, Nol. Too many maybes.'

'I think it must have been Blanche. She could have got her friends to lie about the time she left.'

'If she wanted to kill Thierry it still doesn't make sense to kill Hamish and leave him.'

I couldn't quite pull the logic together, yet.

*

DS Steele met us in Sola, a local café/deli which served great coffee. There was no mistaking the way he looked at Livy, but she seemed oblivious. I worried that she was so emotionally exhausted caring for her son, she had no time for other relationships.

I decided to dive straight in after we ordered.

'I believe you had some doubts about the Nicoll case, Detective Sergeant?'

'MUM!' I could feel the glare but avoided her gaze.

He glanced at Livy and gave a kind of half laugh, half cough of surprise before looking at me. 'You don't beat around the bush, Ms Towers, do you?'

'Doesn't seem much point. We all know why we're here.'

Livy opened her mouth, looking at the point of an apology but I cut in. 'This is so important to us, especially to Livy. Any insight would help us...me.'

By the withering look Livy gave me I could see that using her did not go unnoticed.

'Mmm! Yeah, Livy said you'd taken Thierry Nicoll up on his offer to prove him innocent. I have to tell you, Ms Towers...'

'Nolly, please.'

'Okay, and I'm Steve.'

I nodded.

'Okay, Nolly. You've given yourself a mammoth task and I'm not sure if you will have any luck no matter how hard you try.'

'I accept that, but I have to start somewhere, and you did, maybe do, think it wasn't as open and shut as it seemed, didn't you?'

Another glance at Livy. I could see her squirm out of the corner of my eye.

'Okay, it's obvious Livy said something to you. Look it did seem to be an open and shut case, jealousy, drunken rage ending in death.'

'But?'

'Well, please don't repeat this or I'll lose my job.'

I nodded in agreement.

'The Senior Investigating Officer, Detective Inspector Ferguson, he's young. This was his first murder case. He's ambitious; a fast-track officer and very clever, but he's known to cut corners.'

'Okay, what corners did he cut? I think Nicoll can be aggressive, but he is certain he wouldn't kill his friend...or anyone else.'

'He was fuzzy about what exactly happened and that didn't go down well with the jury. With anyone.'

'But he claims he was knocked out. He said his head was pounding. He remembers pulling out the shard which was like a dagger and staring at it. Then his wife came in and started screaming.'

The coffees and croissants arrived, and he waited while the waitress put them down in front of us. He watched her go, a thoughtful look on his face.

I continued, 'He didn't have any first aid, wasn't taken to a hospital to check for injuries.'

'He was drunk, Nolly. It looked like a drunken rage.'

'Okay, what about this DI?'

'As I said, he's smart, determined, and mad keen on getting quick results. He's aiming high.' A slight tinge of something crept into his tone. Jealousy? Something in my look must have alerted him to what I was thinking.

'I've seen it before with these ambitious types. I prefer to chase the evidence, build up the facts.' He shrugged. 'That doesn't get you a quick promotion.'

Livy cut in, surprising me. 'You're known for being careful and thorough, that's not a fault.'

Steve smiled at her, transforming his rather plain face. 'Thanks, Livy.' Open admiration in his eyes.

'As you were saying,' I prompted.

'Well, a couple of things that didn't add up, I thought,' expression once again serious. 'For one, the Daum collection is Nicoll's obsession. He's paranoid about security around it; state of the art it is. But it was turned off that night and he swears he set it before going out.'

'It's his passion for that collection that makes me think he wouldn't break anything, much less use it as a weapon.' I observed.

'As you said he was drunk when he came home. Is it possible he forgot that he turned the system off?'

'He swore he remembered coming in and telling Hamish it was off.'

I made a couple of notes before picking up my croissant and taking a bite. Livy had her cup held up to her lips and was looking seriously at me, an inscrutable look on her face.

After taking a huge bite from his pastry and gulping a mouthful of coffee he continued, 'There was another thing. He claimed his wife was having an affair with Hamish Todd, but Ferguson said there was no proof and didn't try to look into it. I thought her alibi could have been checked more thoroughly although her pals swore she was with them until after midnight. But the taxi she claimed dropped her off wasn't traced and that was ignored, brushed aside.' Steve shook his head. He lifted his cup downing the rest of the coffee in one gulp.

'However, she had no blood on her or cuts on her hands and only Nicoll's prints were on the shard. It was strong evidence. The Procurator Fiscal was satisfied and signed off on the case.'

'What about Nicoll's defence?' I asked. 'He said he had a solicitor/advocate who was involved in the case from the start. Why didn't he investigate Blanche's alibi?'

'I think he did. He too was young, and confident, maybe a bit overconfident. He was decent but I think he wasn't long qualified as an advocate and I got the impression he tried to make a good impression and was a bit overwhelmed.' Steve pursed his lips. 'Anyway, he didn't present any proof of an alternative. I seem to recall he gave the impression that he didn't believe the wife was having an affair with Hamish, so he went for the lighter sentence because he was convinced his client was guilty.'

I finished my croissant and coffee, wiping the crumbs from my mouth, a bit unsettled by Livy's determined silence.

'Did you think anyone else could have been there?' I asked Steve, still carefully avoiding her eyes.

'No,' with a definite shake of his head. 'I can't see how there could be. Forensics found no evidence of a break-in.'

Livy drained her cup but left the croissant untouched and stood up. I thanked Steve, profusely, telling him it had been a great help. Outside, I hugged her and left quickly.

Chapter 3

Codile Imports, the Nicoll family business, had large premises near the river. Smart offices and an impressive showroom fronted the warehouse. The receptionist took me through the showroom and out to a small office looking into the warehouse. She offered me a coffee, and left after bringing it to me. From the photos lining the walls, Lil looked tall and well built; more substantial than Thierry who was leaner. I guessed that she took after her father, Colin, a stocky Glaswegian, with a pugnacious look about him. I took the opportunity to nosey around the desk but all it contained were notes and copies of orders, various pieces of paper with scribbles on them. It surprised me that the filing cabinet was unlocked and contained staff info and details. The laptop on the desk, unsurprisingly, was password protected.

'What are you doing?' Lil glared at me from the door.

I swallowed, could feel my face reddening but brazened it out. 'I thought this might be Thierry's office and I am trying to find out more about him.' I moved round to the visitor's chair and sat down, lifting the coffee mug attempting nonchalance.

She walked over to the desk and tapped on the laptop, looking satisfied with what she saw. 'This is my office.' Both her face and voice were angry, aggressive. She had the same tawny eyes as Thierry but in her, they glittered, like a big cat. With her flamboyant Kaftan-style dress and her height, she was imposing and intimidating. 'You claimed to be a private investigator when you called but I couldn't find any reference to you.'

'Eh…I keep under the radar and work on word-of-mouth referrals. It suits me.' *God, where was it coming from?*

'So why take on this case? It's high profile and as soon as word gets out, you'll be a target for the press.'

She was sharp. I needed a diversion.

'The name of the company, "Codile", is very unusual, isn't it?'

'It's an amalgamation of Mum and Dad's names, Colin and Odile. Dad started with a stall in the Barras (a market, something of a Glasgow institution, loved and hated in equal measure). He met my mother while on a holiday to Paris. They married and she came to live in Glasgow. She convinced him to expand into luxury goods from the continent as well as Algeria where her family came from.' Lil's face had relaxed as she spoke, obviously proud of her family's success. Her voice was warm when she mentioned her dad, but not her mum and her nostrils flared a bit when she said 'mother'.

She talked freely about her brother and the trial but was oddly ambiguous when I asked her directly if she thought her brother did it. From some of her comments about Blanche, it was clear there was no love lost between them and it was clear that Lil thought Blanche should have left the family home.

'It's not as if they had a perfect marriage,' she said, spite like icy splinters in her tone. 'I have more right to it than she does. She's a gold digger, only after his money. That was all she ever wanted, but he couldn't see it.'

She would not commit to saying that Blanche was having an affair but admitted it would not surprise her. 'She's always flirting with men and never away from that tennis club even in winter.'

As I was leaving, I noticed a fork-lift driver stop her vehicle, load wobbling in mid-air, staring at me then at Lil.

*

Every court was taken at the Kingsland Tennis Club, with a fair number of spectators shouting encouragement to their friends. Thanks to the helpful receptionist I knew that Blanche regularly played on Tuesdays and Thursdays. I found a quiet spot where I could observe without being seen, and within seconds spotted Blanche playing a doubles game with another woman and two men. When it finished, they headed for the pavilion, and I followed. All four sat at a table with soft drinks laughing and joking, comfortable with each other. Blanche and Tom — her partner — left together and I followed. I tailed them to the Nicoll house and watched them go in.

*

Establishing that Blanche was having an affair with Tom was easy. Not so easy to get proof and find out where he was on the night of the killing. I used the bull-in-the-china shop method of detecting again and went to the house.

Once again Blanche opened the door, scowling when she saw me.

'What do you want?'

'A chat with you...about your affair! With Tom. Can I come in?'

Her face turned white, almost green, but she turned and walked inside. I followed. She stopped in the lounge, turning to face me. 'I don't know what you're talking about.'

'Listen, I know you bring him here and he stays overnight.'

That was a long Tuesday night. This surveillance lark is not easy. Resisting the temptation to climb up to the bedroom when the light went on was easy, particularly as my hip was already seizing up.

I outstared her until she sat or rather slumped down onto one of the white sofas.

'Before you deny it again, I have proof. Timed photos and a video. Hard to explain an overnight stay. And don't bother telling me it started after Hamish's death. I can easily find proof it's been going on for a long time. Thierry accused the wrong man, didn't he?'

The silence stretched. The options whirring around in her brain were almost visible.

'Did you put Tom up to it? Was he supposed to kill Thierry?'

'NO!' the screech made my eardrums vibrate. 'We had nothing to do with it, I swear.'

'But you were together that evening?'

She swallowed, and seemed to shrink. 'Yes,' almost a whisper. Probably, she could see the house and money spinning off into the ether when Thierry found out. And Lil would make big waves to get her out. She took a deep breath, 'and I can prove it.'

'How?'

'Tom keeps the receipts for the hotel we use. We were there that night, they know us.'

It had the ring of truth. So much for my theory.

*

A message from the estate agent appeared on my phone reminding me that I needed to pay the deposit, or I would lose the property. The owner was pushing for it as a gesture of goodwill and claiming there was an overseas interest.

Chapter 4

My second visit to the Bar-L was less stressful. This time I could take in more especially the atmosphere of fear and despair, the smell of old sweat seeming to ooze from the walls. Thierry sighed when I told him about Blanche's affair with her tennis partner but did not seem surprised.

'She's obsessed with tennis, but I thought, wrongly as it turns out, that it was all pals together. And Hamish had the hots for her.' His smile had a hint of sadness. 'But I should have known. He was a true pal, he would never have done that to me.' His tone sounded a bit confessional, but, even so, it surprised me when he continued, words spilling out of him as if looking for release. 'I was bordering on the insane with jealousy. Blanche and I, well you could say it was a stormy marriage. We always fought, but that was part of the attraction, for me anyway.' He studied me, head to one side. 'You know, you do remind me of my mum. She was easy to talk to. I feel I can trust you.'

He told me he recently had some hazy flashbacks and was almost sure he had been hit from behind.

'I was drunk, and I still can't remember much about it except holding that piece of the vase.'

'Did you have serious cuts on your hand?'

'No, just a few scratches. But the vase had shattered, and it was a long thin shard, like a stiletto with a bit of the base still attached...like a handle. That's how I pulled it out.' He shuddered as the recollection hit him.

The confessional mode was catching, and I found myself telling him about Peter and how important the plan was to me. I described the property and my plans. He looked interested and kept nodding.

'Tell me something, Ms Towers...'

'Please, call me Nolly.'

'Mmm, okay...Nolly. Are you really a private eye?'

When I admitted my so-called experience consisted of doing witness statements and writing crime stories, he put his head in his hands.

'But I think I'm making progress, Thierry, and I believe that you are innocent. It must be awful to be locked up knowing you didn't do it. Particularly hard when he was your best friend.'

He lifted his head. 'Yes, it haunts me. We have run together since we were boys. I didn't even get to his funeral.'

'If Blanche did it, I'll find proof. I promise, Thierry, I won't stop.'

'Oh, I can easily believe that.'

He looked down at the table. Visiting time was almost up and I stood, ready to leave.

'Sit down, Nolly, please. Listen, I've been thinking. You get plenty of time to do that here.'

God, was he going to ask me to help him break out?

'What you told me about your grandson and your plan is, well … inspiring. At your age…' noting my frown he half-smiled. 'Not that you're old. Anyway, being here has made me think a lot about my life and what I've done with it so far. I've been so caught up in expanding the business, getting somewhere, making money. Now, it doesn't seem to mean that much. I mean, well my marriage is over and I've no kids.'

The guard called for time up and people around us were leaving which appeared to galvanise him. 'What I want to say is, I'll fund you, right now.'

'What?'

'I'll come in… as a silent partner.'

Speech, for once, failed me and he grinned at my expression A road to Damascus moment? I'd take it!

'I do have something of a vested interest,' he added. 'I've always been obsessive, I'm probably on the autistic spectrum. One of the things I've always struggled with is food. Mum was a great cook, but I couldn't eat any of it. Drove her mad when I only wanted KFC or sausage rolls.'

'But is it possible for you to do that, invest and be a silent partner?'

'Yes, I can set up a third-party mandate with my solicitor. It's allowed under prisoners' rights. I set limits and can carry out transactions, pay bills etcetera. I must do it by post but otherwise, it isn't a problem. It means you can go ahead So?' looking enquiringly at me. 'Are you up for it?'

I must have looked like Noddy the dog.

Outside, I found myself shivering, glad to be free and enjoy the beautiful spring outside. It seemed that overnight the trees had gone from winter skeletal trunks and bony branches to forty shades of green. The cherry blossoms too had bloomed and were clothed in delicate pink flowers in contrast to their honey-coloured leaves. How awful it must be not to see the trees and walk free, doubly so when you were innocent. A mixture of elation, pity and dread threaded through me. The euphoria over Thierry's offer was tinged with pity for him, locked up, with his innocence depending on a slightly lame and possibly rather crazy woman.

*

Rob waved from his window and arrived at the conservatory a few minutes later. Over coffee, we talked about the case. Who disarmed the alarm that Thierry was adamant was off when he arrived home? If it was not Blanche, then who? A random thief? Unlikely as nothing was stolen. He could have been disturbed but why knock Thierry out and kill Hamish?

For some reason, I did not tell him about my silent partner.

Chapter 5

The caller identified himself as Andy Frew, the manager who was sacked from Codile's. He had worked at the firm for years, so knew a lot about what went on. His partner, the fork-lift driver I noticed staring as I left, told him about me.

During his time there he had witnessed other furious rows between Lil and Thierry, not just the one they had when Thierry reinstated him. Apparently, she had a ferocious temper and lashed out physically at a warehouseman who accidentally smashed a valuable consignment. Thierry had compensated the man, who had threatened to bring in the police. According to Andy, Lil never forgot when she was wronged and could hold a grudge over trivial things.

Strange that she had not been considered a suspect, although it probably pointed more to Ferguson being blinkered about Thierry's guilt and hell-bent on proving it.

I had to go back to the crime scene. Blanche would be at the tennis club, and I had no idea what I was looking for but had to start somewhere. The side gate was unlocked, and the gardener was busy cutting a hedge.

As I walked towards him, a woman came out of the house. She informed me that she was the cleaner and part-time cook, and that Mrs Nicoll was not at home. The gardener, whose name I discovered was Peter, told her who I was. Like him, she made it clear she did not like Blanche and talked freely. She knew about her affair and said that Lil was not welcome since Thierry had been in prison, giving me the impression that they hated each other. She had noticed nothing different about the house when she was allowed back.

You didn't see Mrs Kennedy around here shortly after the murder?' I asked. 'Or any sign that she had been in the house?'

'No, I heard Mrs Nicoll on the phone shouting. She told her she wasn't welcome. It was her house now.'

I turned again to the gardener. 'Please think hard. Did you notice anything different, funny?'

'Funny?' he looked puzzled.

'Something that shouldn't be there?' I knew my voice sounded desperate.

He shook his head. 'It's nearly winter so I only here to do...' He searched for the word.

'Maintenance?' I suggested.

'Yes, gather leaves, cut a little,' indicating the bushes and trees.

'You didn't see anything broken? Unusual?' he looked even more puzzled. 'Different! Something you didn't expect?'

He shook his head, mouth pursed up, then paused and lifted his finger in a eureka moment. 'The glove.'

'What?'

'I forget. Until now.'

He led me to the shed, went inside and rummaged around for ages.

'Ah!' He pulled out a glove hidden by various bottles and tins on a shelf in a dusty corner behind some tools. As he handed it to me, he said, 'I think belongs to Mrs Nicoll but forget. It was under bush, near French windows.'

'How long after the killing?' I asked.

'Week… maybe two.' He shook his head. 'Not sure, maybe longer.'

It was a woman's black leather glove, right-handed and large, with an expensive label tucked inside. A tingle of adrenaline ran through me when I noticed what looked like scratches in the palm and a dark, stiff-looking stain, like blood. I knew enough about forensics to hold it with a tissue and wrap it in a few more.

As I was hurrying to my car, parked near the house, a man hallooed me.

'You lookin' fur Blanche? Goes tae tennis on Tuesdays and Thursdays.'

Tommy Dowds lived across the road in a much smaller house than the Nicolls'. He was garrulous and nosey. 'You a friend?' he asked.

I gave a non-committal nod and a murmur of agree-ment.

'Terrible business about Thierry,' he went on. 'Ah liked him. He always chatted to me, unlike Blanche. Eh, no offence like.'

'None taken,' I said, finding it difficult to hide my delight at finding a possible source of information.

'She looked down her nose at me. Ah've got the wrang accent for her refined taste.'

He did have a broad Glasgow accent and his scruffy hoodie and battered trainers would not go down well with Blanche, I suspected, although the hoodie had a designer logo, and the trainers were an expensive make.

'I don't suppose you saw anything that night?' I asked.

'Aye! Ah did. This is a quiet area, and we notice strangers. Ah was walking Alfie, he's ma dug, aboot tae cross back tae ma side when someone came running oot o' the wee side gate. Strange cos Ah knew Thierry and Blanche were oot. Whoever it was hud parked the car further alang. Got a look at it as it took aff like a bat oot o' hell.'

'Did the police ask you about this?'

'Naw, Ah wis away early the next mornin'. Aff fur a long winter cruise. Anyway, I didn't think it mattered when Ah read aboot the case. "Open and shut" the polis seemed to think. Shame it came to that. They were great friends.'

'You knew Hamish?'

'Awe, no' well but met them occasionally in the Wally Arms, it's our local like, and we had a pint the gither. Just shows you what jealousy...and booze...can dae, eh?'

'Was it a man or a woman?'

'Whit?'

'Running away that night. Was it a man or woman?'

He puffed his lips and exhaled. 'That's the thing, it could have been either. Same height as me, about five-eight but it was one of they dreary November nights, kinda misty, murky. Glad tae get away from it wi' the wife to sunshine and cocktails by the pool. Oh, and he or she was wearing dark clothes.

'That's not much to go on.'

He was staring curiously at me. 'Who ur ye? Ye're not a friend of Blanche's.'

When I said Thierry had hired me, he smiled broadly. 'That's great. They said it was a drunken fight, but he never seemed the type tae me. Hope ye find oot who did it.'

'So do I but I need to find new evidence and the description doesn't help much. I don't suppose you noticed anything else. The number plate for example?'

'Naw, sorry, too far away. Did notice the smell though?'

'The smell?'

'Scent, I suppose you should call it. Kinda musky... but you know nowadays cannae really tell the men's from the women's, can ye? But Ah would bet it was a wummin. And the car was a beamer...dark, maybe blue...or black.'

*

When I got home, Rob deflated my excitement by reminding me if I did not go to the police with the glove, it would possibly be inadmissible. He pointed out I should have left it in the shed and called the police. Also, it could have been there for weeks, from an earlier visit by Lil. We disagreed heatedly, ending in Rob leaving when I told him I intended to phone a contact I had in a lab — the daughter of a friend — and ask her as a favour if she would process the glove. Unfortunately, she had left for the night, and I paced around restlessly. Adrenaline was bouncing through my veins making my body tingle from fingertips to toes. I needed release and went for a long walk to calm myself.

*

I walked for a couple of hours, and by the time I came back across the Snuff Mill Bridge it was overcast and dark. The only streetlight was high and almost obscured by the trees.

I had no warning of whoever came at me from behind, hoisting me up and trying to topple me over. My feet were off the ground, and I was flailing around. The river was in spate, I could hear the water rushing along forty feet below. My attacker was strong. I still held the stick I used for my walks and tried uselessly to hit him. It clattered onto the road. Wobbling, trying desperately to keep my balance, get my feet back onto the road while scrabbling to get a hold on the wall, I was losing the battle when someone shouted.

'Hey! Stop!' and just as suddenly as he had grabbed me, my attacker let go. Rob barely managed to catch me around the knees, or I would have gone over. We both collapsed against the wall, breathless and gasping. My assailant ran off and disappeared round the bend leaving only a musky scent lingering in the air.

Chapter 6.

Apart from scraped hands, sore ribs, and torn trousers, thankfully, I had no serious injuries, although my ankle throbbed. Rob had seen me going for a walk and watched for my return. He ran out when he saw two dark shapes wrestling on the bridge. All he could be sure of was that the attacker wore a dark hoodie.

Livy joined in his fury at what they saw as my stubbornness. They raged at me for putting myself in so much danger for nothing. Livy, like Rob, thought I was clutching at straws with the glove and stories of the sister's temper and snorted in contempt when I mentioned musky scent.

'I'm sorry, I am. I know you're both worried and believe me I feel pretty shaken up...and worried. But I am not giving up and I have two good reasons not to.'

'What are they, Mum?'

'Firstly, I'm convinced Thierry is innocent. It's highly possible that Lil attacked him and killed Hamish.'

'Why?'

'I don't know, but I am going to get proof.'

Both stared at me, anger changing to confusion.

'What's the second reason, Mum?'

I took a deep breath, forgetting the sore ribs. 'Ouch! Thierry is investing in the centre. It's already in motion. He'll advance the deposit first.'

Livy's voice came out in a wail that tore at my heart. 'I don't believe you, Mum, this is madness. What if you don't get proof. And what if it was him?'

'I don't think so. Lil has a violent temper and was never considered a suspect. No one else was. I am not giving up until I get Thierry released.'

Fortunately, Livy had to leave soon after, having left Peter with a neighbour who occasionally sat in when he was asleep. She left after giving me a token hug.

Rob came and sat beside me on the sofa where I was lying. Gently, he changed the cool compress on my ankle and said he understood how driven I felt, he would feel the same. He stroked my hair and looked on the point of kissing me, but I held up my hand.

'Give me time, Rob,' I pleaded. 'I'm not ready to take on any more emotional baggage. My head is full of proving his innocence and plans for the centre. They are dominating everything I do.'

*

A couple of days later, the manager from Codile, Andy Frew, and his partner Tracey met me in the café Sola. He showed me a video recording on his phone of the row between Lil and Thierry after he reinstated Andy. The sound was something of a babble with only occasional words and phrases clear although it was easy to identify Lil's voice screaming at Thierry who was pale but calm. At one point she lifted her hand to hit him, but he grabbed it, stopping her in mid-blow. He noticed the blinds were open and he crossed the office, closed them and from then on it was mostly the sound of Lil's voice berating Thierry.

Tracey also said she believed Lil was taking large orders that did not go through the books although she had no proof, it was based on warehouse gossip.

*

True to his word Thierry had transferred funds through Gerry Naismith, his solicitor and I had paid the deposit so the sale was going ahead smoothly, well as smoothly as a brand-new not-for-profit company being set up could go. I met Gerry, the solicitor as well as Thierry's accountant and discussed the business plan that Rob had worked out for me.

Rob was keen to see the house and grounds, so we took Peter. Rob was impressed and Peter loved it. Livy could not come as she was in Edinburgh on police business, she said.

*

Thierry pooh-poohed the whole idea of Lil being responsible when I spoke to him on the phone and was defensive about his big sister.

'She wouldn't attack me,' he insisted. 'And kill Hamish…no way. I know all about her temper, but it blows over.'

'What about if she were cornered? How would she react? On Andy's video, she looks extremely violent.'

'Yes, I agree we did fight, but we had lots of them.'

'But does she hold grudges? Over trivial things? How much did she resent you inheriting the business?'

The line went silent apart from static whistling through it.

'Have the arguments and fights got worse since your mother died?'

The pause was so long I thought we were disconnected.

'Yes, I suppose so. There have been some serious incidents. But attack me? Kill Hamish? No!'

I got it. Thinking the big sister you grew up with, looked up to, could attack you and kill your best friend must be extremely difficult to believe.

'Another thing, Thierry, is it possible Lil is taking orders and they don't show in the books?'

'I don't think so, she wouldn't do that,' but his voice was subdued, hesitant.

Chapter 7

Reluctantly, my contact in the lab had agreed to examine the glove and keep it under the radar. The suspense was killing me while I waited for the results. One positive development was that DCI Ferguson had been promoted to a job in the Met, and after a lot of persuasion, DS Steele managed to get put in charge of a limited new investigation into a possible miscarriage of justice. According to Livy, he was painstakingly going through all the evidence again. I passed on the information from Andy, the manager, plus the conversation with the neighbour, but some lingering distrust made me hold back about finding the glove. The musky scent I kept to myself.

*

Lil's son in Australia was contacted and, although cagey about it, admitted his mother did have a violent temper and mood swings; other employees confirmed unfair and harsh treatment but had kept quiet, afraid of losing their jobs. Steele also tracked down an old neighbour of Lil's who moved away because she constantly made life a misery for his family for a supposed slight.

But these were all character-related as Livy reminded me. There was no evidence that she was in the house that night or that she killed Hamish. Everything rested on the glove.

*

Peter surprised me by asking when we were going to *His House* as he called it and I took him for another visit this time with Livy. The builders had started the renovations and Livy wandered around, mouth open, eyes glowing. When she threw her arms around me whispering, 'I get it, Mum, I finally do get it,' my heart swelled with love. I just hoped we would get it.

*

The wait was interminable and when the call finally came from my contact my nerves were shredded. Lil had not been charged but DS Steele had invited her into the station and questioned her which at least showed the police were taking it seriously. I hoped that with that hanging over her I would be safe from another attack but found myself anxiously looking round every time I stepped outside. Walks over the bridge were out. Often, I would find myself staring at it, paranoid that she would jump up like a kind of weird bogey woman. Mostly I kept the blinds partially closed, blocking it out.

*

Tess McLeod, my contact at the lab, was waiting for us. She led us to a quiet office. DS Steele's face was serious as I turned to him. 'I asked you here so that you could hear first-hand what Tess found out about the glove, Steve.'

Tess held up her hand, 'This wasn't just me, Nolly. I had to call in a few favours from a different specialist to get all the tests done.'

She handed us several printed reports and summarised what they had found.

In essence, the evidence they found exceeded anything I hoped for. The glove was indeed expensive, and it was possible it could be traced back through the company or the shop which stocked them, to the buyer. Steele took careful note of that. They had found tiny fragments of glass and a human bloodstain on it. Also, the slight cut on the palm contained particles of the same glass.

*

DS Steele went straight to a senior officer with the reports and the glove, and I was summoned to Chief Superintendent Simon Wallace's office. It was both impressive and intimidating. Livy told me that he was equally revered and hated by his staff; a hard taskmaster and known to surround himself with sycophants.

DI Ferguson was a protégé of his, and it was rumoured that Wallace was furious that an upstart, unknown civilian was stirring up trouble, casting doubts on a rock-solid case. He was a big man, running a bit to fat but fit-looking, with steel-grey hair, hard blue eyes, an immaculate uniform, and a stiff shirt collar so white it dazzled.

He did not invite me to sit. Introductions were minimal. DS Steele stood by the door.

'Do you know you face serious charges, Ms Towers? Withholding evidence illegally obtained being one of them.'

The tone of his voice and his rudeness wiped away any awe I felt.

'I thought you called me in to thank me!' Pleased that I spoke without a quaver. 'The police and our judiciary incarcerated an innocent man. Thanks to me we have new evidence. At the very least I deserve thanks.'

His face took on a slight tinge of purple and he looked as if the dazzling collar suddenly became a bit tight.

'For your information,' I continued, temper well up now, 'the glove was not acquired illegally.' I'd checked what private investigators were allowed to do, thankfully. 'I am employed as a private investigator and entitled to gather evidence which helps my client.'

'You went to Nicoll's house when Mrs Nicoll was out and took the glove from her premises.' He positively thundered. 'That is illegal.'

'It would be if Mrs Nicoll owned the house...' I paused for effect. 'But she doesn't. Mister Nicoll owns it, and he has permitted me to investigate his wrongful verdict.'

The Chief Super glared past me at DS Steele, and I felt a twinge of guilt that I had been so blunt, letting my quick temper take over again.

'Is this true?' I glanced back at DS Steele who looked surprisingly unperturbed.

'Yes sir.

The CS struggled to swallow before uttering a grudging apology and a barely acceptable thank you.

Chapter 8

I watched the staff leaving and the warehouse lights go out before I walked through to Lil's office in Codile. She was engrossed in the laptop and looked up in surprise which quickly turned to anger when I opened the door.

'What d'you think you're playing at barging in here? Thierry might have hired you, but I run this business.'

'Yes, exactly what you wanted isn't it?'

'What are you on about? You know what, get out!'

'What happened that night? Why did you go to Thierry's house?'

She stood up and came round the desk until she was inches from me. 'Get out,' she hissed.

'You stabbed Hamish, didn't you?' I persisted.

Her eyes narrowed, something dark and deadly lurking in them. I felt a frisson of fear run through me and in that instant was convinced she did it.

This could go horribly wrong...a bit like baiting a bear.

'WHAT! You're mad! What are you on about? Is this a crazy ploy to get the money?'

I kept pushing, ignoring the rising fear flooding me. 'You've always resented Thierry, haven't you? The favoured son? What pushed you over the edge? His going over your head? Reinstating Andy?'

Her breathing quickened, her eyes narrowed to slits, face contorting into a mask of fury.

'SHUT UP! YOU DON'T KNOW WHAT YOU'RE TALKING ABOUT?'

'Did you lose a glove the night you killed Hamish? After knocking Thierry out?'

A momentary flash of surprise. Shock, then recognition widened her eyes.

'The police have it now. It will prove you were there and murdered Hamish.'

With a suddenness that took me completely by surprise, she grabbed my neck. She was big and strong, and I fell back across her desk, her fingers clutching at my throat squeezing, squeezing. Instinct made me grab at her hands before a tiny bit of reason warned me it would not work. I threw myself further back and brought up my knee, at the same time poking her hard in the eye which made her head jerk back and knocked her a little off-balance, but not enough for her to let go of my throat although the pressure eased enough for me to grab a morsel of air before she grunted and squeezed harder.

Over and over, she muttered in a grunting voice. 'Why couldn't he just leave it?'

Stars and blackness filled my vision and consciousness started to fade. Ironically, that musky scent hit me, perhaps the last thing I would ever be aware of in this life.

With a loud rumble the forklift truck came crashing through the door, Rob at the controls. The door crashed onto us, pushing the desk backwards and we fell, her weight heavy on me, hands still round my throat. I have only a hazy recollection of the chaos that followed. Apparently, Rob jumped out and launched himself at Lil who was still trying to choke the life out of me. The police arrived and pulled the two of them apart as I lay, barely conscious, gasping for breath, on the floor. Lil was screaming that I had attacked her, and she was defending herself.

DS Steele was bending over me asking if I was OK. Officers were holding Rob and Lil who was still yelling. We were all taken to the police station although Rob and I were released within a couple of hours. I was cautioned that charges might be brought against me. Lil was charged and detained.

A white-faced Livy picked us up. Her silence unnerved me, maybe this time I had gone too far. She stopped outside the house but when we got out, she put the car in gear and drove off without a word. Rob looked exhausted and I felt numb.

'I didn't know you followed me,' I said.

'I know you, Nolly. Saying you were going for a chat with her didn't convince me. I knew you would try something crazy so I followed and phoned DS Steele from the car.'

'I was recording it,' I murmured, weakly.

He gave me a withering look, saw me to the front door and left.

Inside the house felt cold, abandoned. What had I achieved? At this point, I thought I had screwed the whole thing up. My darling daughter could not even speak to me and my best friend who came to my rescue like a knight of old, forklift truck replacing a horse, had left me alone.

*

The following day, I went to Livy's flat when she came off an early shift. Peter was still at school. She looked so exhausted and pale, my heart went out to her.

'I'm so sorry, Livy. I know I went too far.'

'Mum, you could have been killed. This is too much for you, give it up, please.' She started to cry, sobbing uncontrollably. In all the years she had struggled to come to terms with Peter's autism and learning how to cope with it, I had never seen her like this. I held her close, in tears myself.

'I can't give up now, Livy. I'm so close.'

She pulled away, her tear-streaked face an accusation. 'Mum, I know how hard it is for you to give up on anything, but the police will handle it now.'

'Like they did the first time. A wrongful murder conviction on Ferguson's record won't go down well, it could block more promotions. Think about it, Liv. He's the chief super's man so Wallace will try to block or stall for as long as possible. There are lots of ways he could do it and make the investigation drag on for years. I needed to take action, Liv, persuade them there's been a miscarriage of justice.' She sat slumped in the chair, shaking her head. I knelt beside her, took her hands.

'I need to see it through, Livy, please support me. I thought she might confess…how wrong that was, eh?'

'Oh, Mum, how do you get yourself into these situations?'

'They haven't all been disastrous, Liv. Remember the greenhouse?'

A slight smile appeared, 'Yes, and that cost you a fractured hip and left you with a limp.'

My hip twinged in agreement.

Chapter 9

Thierry was released rapidly because of several factors beginning with the publicity around the attack and Lil being charged with assault. The case became high profile when it was taken up by the charity, Miscarriages of Justice. This allied to the painstaking work of DS Steele and his small team combined to convince the Procurator to treat the case as a matter of urgency.

Working tirelessly, DS Steele established that the glove was hers, particles of the glass were found in her car and on a winter coat of hers, proving she had been in the house that night. One lucky find was a slightly larger fragment of glass found at the back of the wardrobe where her coat hung. A troll of CCTV images found photos of her dark blue BMW going towards the house earlier that evening and going back by the same route shortly after the time of the murder. Along with other circumstantial evidence such as the neighbour's statement it was considered strong enough to release Thierry and arrest Lil. She denied being there or killing

Hamish but had no alibi, claiming she stayed at home all evening.

*

Hallowe'en was approaching fast. Strangely enough for a boy as reserved as Peter, he loved dressing up as Batman, his favourite superhero. I loved it almost as much and decorated the house with cobwebs and lanterns, ghoulish skulls, and skeletons. Predictably, I was a witch. At Peter's insistence, Livy was a Disney princess and Rob was a pirate who had to shout, 'Ahoy me Mateys!' every time a guiser came to the door. I still found the American expression, 'Trick or Treat,' a bit ridiculous though it probably sounded better than, 'Anything for my Hallowe'en,' when I was young.

Dooking for apples was in full swing with lots of laughing in the background when I opened the door expecting more guisers. Thierry stood there with a small parcel held out to me. Inside were the keys to the centre which was fast nearing completion thanks to his expertise and, of course, his money.

He joined in the fun and told a couple of funny jokes, accepting the goodie bag and diving straight into the sweets. As Livy led the local kids to the door, he asked if he could have a word in private. Rob quietly slipped away before I could stop him.

'I saw Lil,' he said. 'I think she is going to confess.' The sadness on his face was heartbreaking and I reached out and took his hand. 'She needs help, Nolly. I never knew how deeply she resented me...hated me really.' He told me about his upbringing, the favoured son, and how Lil felt overlooked in every way after he appeared. Her hatred and resentment boiled up inside her for years and her temper which he knew could be unstable worsened.

'She was full of anger about Andy, felt as if I had taken the last piece of power, the only piece, away from her when I reinstated him. She nursed it and nursed it until it poisoned her whole being. One of the things she resented was that I got not only the house but the Daum collection. I forgot she had a key and that night she let herself in, switched off the alarm and took out the vase Mum and I loved most. She was sitting on the sofa, stewing, when we came in. I rushed over to the cabinet, and she said a red mist filled her mind. She stood up and smashed the vase over my head.'

He had to stop at this point. Livy had come in, noted what was happening and quietly took Peter upstairs. I poured Thierry a mug of coffee laced with whisky, and he gulped down a big mouthful.

'It's okay, Thierry, you don't have to tell me any more.'

'I owe it to you, Nolly. Only after I collapsed did she see Hamish swaying, staring at her, obviously very drunk. She says she panicked, picked up the shard and stabbed him with it. Then she heard Blanche coming in and ran to the French doors, letting herself out and running out by the side gate. When she fumbled with the French door, she took off her glove and must have dropped it outside.'

He shuddered, eyes full of tears. I put my arm around him, feeling his sadness, lost for words.

Epilogue.

Thierry performed an opening ceremony and we let Peter cut a ribbon at the doorway to Peter's House. It was the proudest moment of my life. Between us, Thierry and I had fitted out special rooms, employed expert staff and done all the million and one things to bring the centre to a state of excellence. We even had horses, but I knew nothing about them, so Thierry took on the responsibility. It looked as if he was going to be a hands-on partner.

DS Steve Steele was there or rather, DI Steele as he was now, a reward for his sterling work and dedication. Livy stood beside him. They were an item now, and luckily Peter was getting over his wariness and starting to accept him.

I had agreed to a holiday with Rob with no strings and was not sure where it would take us.

A buffet was laid on in the grand hall, with specially catered food for the autistic kids we had invited with their parents. Thierry came up to me as I stood beaming; I could not get the smile off my face. He handed me a beautifully wrapped present. Inside was an amazing teal coloured Daum vase. The card with it read that it was a limited edition. The design incorporated features of an African mask with Art Deco influences.

'I hope this will always remind you of me, Nolly. Thank you from the bottom of my heart.'

The Painting

Claire Miller

The Painting

Anna just managed to stop the scream before she woke up. Tears drenched her cheeks. Her heart pounded in her chest.

She was shaking and soaked in sweat. Her breaths came in short sharp bursts. Her eyes darted around the room taking in her surroundings. The last few notes of the harp music faded as her dream disappeared from her memory.

Rattled she got out of bed, walked over to the window and opened the curtains. *Was she really where she thought she was?* The gardens of Rosewood Manor greeted her. She breathed a sigh of relief. She was safe.

She knew she couldn't tell her aunt and uncle about this. Normally, at this time of year, they kept her close to them. Any suspicion of her lack of control would have her being ordered back into the care of the doctors again. Her memory of her journey from chaos to control was one that she didn't want to repeat.

The only reason she was at Rosewood Manor was because she had reassured them that she was handling everything and capable of valuing the objects for the upcoming charity auction at Thompson Auctioneers. It was important to her and her uncle.

She wanted to value the objects, at Carlton Hall, the nearby stately home, to contribute to an important cause.

Jumping as the phone rang beside the bed, she quickly picking up the receiver to protect her jangling nerves.

'Hello, Anna, this is the wake-up call that you requested.' It was, Sue, the guest house owner.

'Thanks.'

'Did you sleep well?'

'I had an excellent night's sleep, thank you.'

'Great, I'll see you at breakfast.'

She put the receiver on the phone and took a deep breath. She had plenty of time to collect herself and look forward to an exciting day. No one must know what had happened.

It took longer than she had planned to get from her bedroom to the dining room. There were so many interesting objects and paintings to look at.

One small painting in particular caught her attention by the dining room. A golden harp stood in the middle of a room with a burgundy wall behind it. On either side of the wall were doors which opened out onto a garden. The sun coming into the room was casting shadows across the floor in front of the harp. Velvet curtains, matching the walls, draped across the edges of the doors. She wondered if the harp sounded anything like the harp music she'd heard in her dream.

'It's a beautiful painting, isn't it,' a voice said beside her.

She jumped and turned to see Sue, standing beside her, a thoughtful look on her face. 'I'm sorry, Anna; I didn't mean to give you a fright.'

'I was engrossed in the picture that's all. I forget about everything else when I am studying paintings. I love the detail in the painting. Who is the artist?

'The daughter of the family, who originally owned Rosewood Manor. I can tell you all about her if you like but it might be better if I did that later. You don't have a lot of time to eat your breakfast if you want to be at Carlton Hall on time. It was 9am you had to be there wasn't it?'

Anna looked at her watch, remembering she'd been talking to Sue when she'd checked-in the previous day, then smiled gratefully at her.

'I took longer than I expected getting from my bedroom to the dining room. There are so many fascinating objects and pieces of art to look at. Thanks for reminding me about the time.'

Sue laughed. 'I thought you might. There is an extensive collection of antiques in Rosewood Manor. I can give you a guided tour of Rosewood Manor when you get back from Carlton Hall if you'd like.'

'Thanks, I'll look forward to that.'

Anna took a moment to focus her mind as she sat in her car outside Carlton Hall. Her uncle had taught her everything she knew about antiques and valuing them. Her specialist knowledge was in paintings.

Every time she valued something she felt that she was thanking him and her aunt for taking her in and looking after her. Her mind now fully focused on a job she got out of the car.

She returned to Rosewood Manor tired but happy in the afternoon. It had been a good day. The choice of objects had been wonderful. She had catalogued and valued them; making notes on any research that needed to be done when she got back to the auction house.

Mr Chisholm, the owner of Carlton Hall, had also offered her a special family item. She knew her uncle would be pleased with her.

Sue was booking in another guest, a medium height dark-haired man, when Anna walked into the entrance of Rosewood Manor. He smiled at her before he took his key and walked away to find his room.

'I'll be with you in 10 minutes,' Sue said when Anna approached the reception desk.

'Thanks, I've got to phone my uncle. I'll come back when I've done that.'

'Great, I'll see you then.'

Anna steeled herself before she picked up the phone in her bedroom to talk to her uncle. She knew what the first question was going to be.

'How did you sleep?' her uncle asked.

'Very well, thank you.'

There was a moment of silence on the other end of the phone. She could tell he was deciding whether to believe her or not. She waited for him to speak. If she spoke to him too quickly he would think she was trying to distract him. She knew this from experience.

'How did you get on at Carlton Hall?' he asked eventually.

After she had told him about everything she'd listed and the special family item that Mr Chisholm had offered to her he congratulated her and ended the call.

She breathed a huge sigh of relief glad that the phone call was over. She was one more day closer to the questions being stopped, for another year.

Now to find Sue and get the promised guided tour. Sue was waiting by the painting for her. 'There you are, Anna, I thought we'd start here.'

'Great, I am looking forward to hearing all about the artist. The detail is so realistic.'

Sue looked worried. 'The story behind this painting is sad. Grace, the owner's daughter, was forced by her uncle to stop playing the harp. The only way she had to remember her music was to paint this picture. The harp disappeared from the house shortly after this painting was created.'

Anna took another look at the painting. 'She obviously loved the harp. I can almost imagine I could hear it being played.'

Sue looked sharply at her. 'Did you hear harp music when you slept last night?'

Anna stared at the guest house owner in shock. *How could she have known this?*

Taking a slow breath, as she'd been taught to calm herself, she thought about how to answer this question. If she admitted she'd heard the harp playing she would have to acknowledge to herself her true feelings.

She couldn't do this. She had spent years building walls around her heart. Walls which if breached would let a flood out. She was in control and that was the way it was going to stay.

As she was about to answer the question, having thought up an answer, Sue gently but firmly took hold of her arm and propelled her up the stairs and along the corridor to the library.

Anna knew where she was going because she had found the library when she had been exploring Rosewood Manor between arriving and dinner yesterday evening. Sue shut the door with a firm click. Anna looked at the guest house owner alarmed by the serious expression on her face.

'I was listening to classical music in the car on the way here...' she started to say.

'Many guests look at Grace's painting, few actually "see" it or mention imagining they can hear the harp playing. Grace only lets guests who need her help really "see" her painting.'

Anna was trying to make sense of what she'd heard when Sue continued, 'Previous guests have told me they have "heard" harp music, when they have contacted me and asked me to thank Grace for warning them of the danger they have survived. Other guests have not been so lucky. The reports in the papers have all mentioned harp music.'

Sue paused before saying, 'You are in danger.'

Anna stared at Sue bewildered. A silent scream echoed in her head. She closed her eyes, trying not to remember her aunt's and uncle's concerned faces. After several controlled breathes, she opened them to see Sue staring intently at her.

'Come and meet Grace.'

Sue turned her round and pointed to a large portrait of a young girl displayed on a stand in the corner of the room. Despite the chills racing through her Anna got closer to the portrait. Her natural curiosity and love for paintings took over.

She saw a young girl with fair hair elegantly pinned up and a gentle smile, on her pretty face, standing in a garden surrounded by blooming rose bushes. Grace was wearing a long cream dress with a high neck and full-length sleeves, lace detail decorated the top layer of material and a satin sash highlighted the waist. The brush strokes were exquisite, and the colour choices were so vibrant.

'Amazing,' Anna said to herself, tracing the lines of the dress with her fingers.

She turned to look at Sue. 'Who painted this?'

'Grace's mother, she was an excellent artist and musician. She played the harp, like Grace, and toured giving concerts, with Grace's dad. He was a musician too.'

Anna slowly counted backwards from 10 to 1 in her head. At 1 she could think again.

She decided not to listen to the classical music on the way home in the car, it would hurt too much. She needed to distance herself. 'Where was the portrait painted?'

'In Rosewood Manor's garden.'

The garden Anna could see from her bedroom. Some fresh air sounded like what she needed just now. 'I have to see it; I didn't have time to go into it yesterday.'

Sue smiled at her. 'I'll take you there now. I have something to give you first that you might want to read.'

She went to a shelf by the door and pulled a book out then gave it to Anna.

'*Rosewood Manor- An Illustrated History,*' Anna read.

'It was written by one of Rosewood Manor's former owners. I'm sure you'll enjoy reading it.'

Anna stroked the beautifully bound leather cover. She opened the book.

'Come on,' Sue said laughing a little, 'I'll show you where you can read it in the garden, there's plenty of time before dinner.'

Following Sue to the lounge Anna gasped when she realised it seemed familiar to her.'This is where...'

'Yes,' said Sue, 'this is the background to Grace's harp painting. She loved this room.'

'I can see why,' Anna said admiring the views through the two sets of doors that led out to the garden.

Sue took her to the seats, surrounded by fragrant rose bushes, in the garden. Anna gratefully took a few deep breaths of fresh air and then settled down to read the book.

Eagerly she looked at the pictures of the objects and paintings in Rosewood Manor and read the history of each.

The story behind an object fascinated her. She loved imagining who was involved in the journey between an object being created and ending up in its final resting place. The information helped her learn so much about what was actually happening at the time, the people involved and the places where everything was taking place.

She was just about to read about Grace's portrait when she realised it was time for the evening meal. Reluctantly she closed the book. She would continue reading it after dinner.

The other guest smiled at her, as she left the dining room, as soon as she had finished her meal. She was eager to carry on reading the book.

Settling into a chair, in her bedroom, she opened the book at the page where Grace's portrait was and read the notes on the opposite page.

'Lucy Carson painted many portraits but always said her favourite was the one she painted of her daughter Grace.'

Anna smiled as she looked at the picture, Grace looked so happy.

'I would have loved to know you,' she said out loud.

'I'd like to know you too,' a voice said.

She looked around the room startled. There wasn't anyone else in the room. She waited for a few moments but the only sound in the room was her heart beating loudly. She focused on the book and carried on reading.

'This was the last painting Lucy ever produced. Sadly, she died shortly after the portrait's completion. Her talent will be greatly missed.'

Anna's breath stuck in her throat; she felt the familiar feelings of panic beginning to build in her body.

She snapped the book shut, put it on the table beside her, then squeezed her hands into two tight fists. Her nails dug into the palms of her hands. She concentrated on the pain forcing any other thoughts out of her head.

It was several minutes before she was happy she had pushed away the unwanted feelings. Her fingers ached with the effort.

Her gaze rested on the book. She'd love to read more of it but couldn't. She'd wait until she was feeling mentally stronger. The walls around her heart needed repaired. She went to bed early hoping sleep would bring some relief.

Her uncle and aunt's faces swam across her mind. She fought to move away but they kept getting closer. She could see the room again where they had put her after the show. Her screams filled the air. She woke up with a jolt. This time she really had screamed out loud. Desperately she waited to see if any footsteps were running along the corridor to her room; frantically trying to think up what she would say if anyone asked her why she had screamed.

Relief flooded her when she realised no one was coming. Normally she managed to hold the scream in. She must be getting too relaxed around others at the moment; she needed to be more careful. She lay shaking in the bed.

'You're not alone,' a voice said.

Her eyes darted around her room. A soft white light began to appear at the end of her bed. The cream material and satin sash of Grace's dress glowing as she stepped forward. Anna blinked then saw just her room. She had to be remembering Lucy's portrait of Grace. It was a very striking image of her.

Her phone rang. She jumped and snatched at the handset attempting to breathe normally.

'Yes.'

'Good morning, you asked me to call you.'

Anna remembered she had asked the guest house owner for the wake-up call again.

'Thanks.'

'It's my pleasure. I hope you had a good night's sleep.'

She was exhausted but said, 'I had a great night's sleep, thanks.'

'Good, I'll see you at breakfast.'

Sinking into the bed, after carefully placing the receiver on the phone, she knew she just had to get through the day. After that she would be in her new flat, all alone, and able to be herself.

Picking up the book she took a last look around her room to make sure that she hadn't left anything behind. She really wanted to read more. She needed to know what had happened to Grace after her mum's death. *Was it possible to carry on living after such an event?*

She practised her smile in the mirror by the bedroom door, after brushing her brown shoulder length hair away from her hazel eyes; no one must know how she was really feeling.

Sue smiled as she came downstairs to breakfast. Anna smiled back hoping she looked happy.

'I've really enjoyed my stay here, thanks for everything. Here's the book back.'

'It's been lovely having you. Please keep the book until you've finished with it.'

She looked at Sue in surprise. It was obviously a valuable book.

'Are you sure?'

'Yes I am. Grace will let you know when it's time for the book to return to Rosewood Manor, let me show you to your table.'

She followed Sue to the dining room not quite sure what to make of what she had just listened to. The image of Grace in her bedroom flashed through her mind. *It hadn't been real, had it?*

Sue stood in the entrance and waved as Anna drove away from Rosewood Manor. Her last words echoing through Anna's mind. 'Listen to Grace, she will look after you.'

Anna had no idea what to make of them.

The other guest had been standing behind Sue, a triumphant look on his face. Anna had briefly seen him reading the guest comment's book before she'd left. She thought he probably got as much pleasure as she did reading the previous guest's comments.

She had written her new address for the first time in the book and remembered a feeling of satisfaction; she was starting a new life, one full of hope and freedom.

Her first stop was her flat where she dropped her bag off, she would unpack later after work, then she headed towards the auction house. Her uncle would be keen to get the paperwork for the charity auction.

She was eager to start the preparation work for the charity auction especially as there was the special family item to sell.

Practising smiling, before she started the short walk to Thompson Auctioneers from her flat, was essential. Her uncle would be watching her every move in the auction house. Even after all the years it paid to be prepared.

Her uncle quickly glanced over her handwritten notes she'd made at Carlton Hall. His concentrated expression the one she had come to know and love after all the years she had known him. He took his job very seriously. He appreciated every item which came through his auction house and always said that the story behind each item was unique and to be celebrated.

'This is great work,' he said smiling at her. 'You've done an excellent job. The vase Mr Chisholm added to the sale will add lots of money to the charity's funds.'

Her uncle was referring to the special family item Mr Chisholm had offered to her to sell along with all the other antiques.

She thought of the beautifully detailed Chinese dragon, dancing amongst small blue flowers, set against the luminous gold background and the blue bands around the base, shoulder and neck of the vase. Her value of £2000 was just an estimate, she fully expected it go for much more than that.

His expression turned serious, she braced herself, for what was about to come. 'Are you sure you are okay?'

She smiled her best smile. 'I am. I promised I'd tell you if I needed help.'

He paused gazing intently at her. 'I'm still not sure we should have let you move into your flat just now. You know I was happy to pay all your costs if you'd agreed to move in after the anniversary.'

She clearly remembered that discussion. Her aunt and uncle had tried their very best to persuade her to stay with them just a little longer when she'd announced all the paperwork for the sale of her flat had been completed. It had taken sometime but eventually she had persuaded them she would be okay on her own. The first night in the flat had been amazing especially as she knew that her aunt and uncle didn't have keys for her flat.

'I know.'

He looked at her for a little longer. She waited; this was what she had to do when her uncle talked to her. He returned the paperwork to her. 'Give Marie the information you need to, I look forward to reading the extra details you learn from your research. I'm sure it will add to the charity auction catalogue. This is Mr Chisholm's first event with us; I have promised him great results.'

Anna gave Marie the information that needed to be typed up then started her research.

Her uncle had to remind her to go to lunch. She was so wrapped up in what she was discovering and had completely forgotten the time.

She was finished her research by the middle of the afternoon. Her exhaustion was catching up with her. After giving Marie her research notes to type up she headed back home, after checking with her uncle that there wasn't anything else to do.

He said he'd get the typed notes from Marie and then be phoning Mr Chisholm later to arrange for the photographer's visit to Carlton Hall. They'd talk tomorrow morning.

She fell fast asleep when she got home, her lack of quality sleep finally catching up with her. It was evening when she woke up. Thankfully her sleep had been music and dream free. She clung on to these rare moments. They were a reminder of what was going to come eventually.

Deciding to unpack her bag before she made herself something to eat, she opened her bag. She was looking forward to putting her belongings away in "her" space.

Grace's harp painting was sitting on the top of her clothes. Anna stared in shock. *How had it got there?* She had to contact Sue. She didn't want her to think she had taken the painting from Rosewood Manor.

She needed the phone number of Rosewood Manor. She couldn't phone Marie, who had booked her into the guest house, as the auction house would be closed now. *What was she going to do?*

Panic was setting in when she remembered that she'd picked up one of the leaflets about Rosewood Manor, which had the phone number on it. She tipped her handbag on the couch and found the leaflet.

Sue picked up the phone on the second ring. 'Rosewood Manor, how can I help you?'

'I'm sorry, Sue,' Anna blurted out, 'I don't know how it happened I really don't.'

'Anna, I take it Grace's painting is in your bag.'

Anna stared at the phone in shock then spoke in a quiet voice. 'How do you know that?'

'The painting has disappeared off the wall at Rosewood Manor. It will reappear when Grace is ready to return.'

Anna felt the blood drain from her face and knew if she looked at herself in a mirror she would be very pale. She sat in silence for a moment.

'Are you there, Anna?'

'What's happening, Sue?'

'Grace is going to help you. Listen to her and everything will be okay.'

Anna was silent again, not sure what to think.

'Anna...' It was Sue again.

'Yes.'

'Trust Grace.' Sue ended the call.

Anna looked around her lounge feeling uncertain and frightened by having her own space for the first time. Harp music began to play. She dropped the phone.

Grace appeared in front of her, in a flash of white light, and picked it up.

'Put my painting on your wall then unpack and eat, I'll talk to you later.'

Grace and the harp music faded away leaving Anna alone. Because she couldn't think of anything else to do, she did as Grace had asked her to.

More harp music alerted her to Grace's re-appearance. She saw Grace playing the harp in the painting then Grace was standing in front of her.

'You're in danger. Please let me help you.'

Shutting her eyes Anna counted to 10 then opened them again. Grace was still there.

'I know the pain you are holding onto. It will take over your life if you keep refusing to deal with it. I know because I had to do this.'

A cry of fear leapt out of her as a brick fell out of the wall around her heart. Her legs gave way. Grace caught her and held her up. She found herself being gently lowered down onto the couch. Grace sat down beside her. She reached out and touched Grace's dress. The material slid gently between her fingers.

'You can't be real,' she whispered.

Grace smiled. 'If you let me help you, I'll heal your heart.'

Anna heard her uncle's voice questioning her asking her if she was okay. She jumped up and glared at Grace. 'I'm in control.'

Even as she said this, she knew it wasn't true but the many years of hiding her pain had made this her automatic response. 'I'm not in danger.'

Grace smoothly rose up off the couch. She smiled at Anna. 'Let me know when you want my help. All I ask in return is that you let go of the past.'

Tears formed in Anna's eyes. She couldn't do that. If she did, she'd be accepting what had happened, her life would fall apart.

Grace began to fade away. 'I'll let you know when the danger is coming, what happens after that is your choice.'

She stared as Grace disappeared. Looking at Grace's painting she saw the harp sitting alone in the room. She wondered if she had just dreamt about Grace being in her lounge. It had to be the lack of sleep.

The book Sue had leant her was sitting on the table by the couch, it opened at the page where Grace's story began.

Anna shut the book she didn't want to know about Grace. The book sprung open at the same page. She shut it again. Once more the pages flipped open. She backed away from the book.

'Read the book,' she heard Grace saying.

She tried to leave the lounge but the door wouldn't open.

'All I ask is that you read my story.'

Inching her way towards the table and the book she glanced at the painting and saw Grace watching her; she gave Anna an encouraging nod of her head.

Her hands shook as she sat on the couch, picked up the book and began to read.

'Grace had a happy childhood until tragedy struck. At the age of 15 her parents were killed in a fire that swept through the hall her parents were performing in.'

She gasped for breath, her control disappearing. Grace appeared beside her again.

'I... can't... read... this...' she said looking at Grace.

Grace wrapped her arms around Anna. A feeling of calm crept slowly through Anna's body. Her breathing changed from ragged, sharp intakes to a smooth, slow flow of air in and out.

'I'll tell you my story.'

Anna struggled to get out of Grace's hold not wanting to experience her difficulty to breathe again. It had taken a long time for her to learn how to control the feelings that triggered this reaction.

Her uncle had only let her start working in the auction house once the doctors had reassured him that she had control. She wanted to keep working.

'I promise to protect you,' Grace said.

To Anna's surprise she found that she no longer felt the need to fight against Grace's hold. Somehow, she knew Grace would keep her safe.

'I don't understand,' she said to herself then looked into Grace's smiling face.

'My uncle became my guardian when my parents died. He married me off to the son of one of his friends. I spent many years hiding my true feelings about my parents' deaths. My uncle only needed a small reason to send me away. He would have lived off my inheritance with my husband and I would be locked away forever.'

Anna listened feeling completely calm.

'Poor health took my uncle and my husband was killed in a hunting accident.'

Anna knew she would normally feel a reaction to what Grace was telling her but at this moment she was content to listen to Grace.

'Family friends, who my uncle had stopped from contacting me, helped me learn to come to terms with my feelings. I found love and was happy for the rest of my life.'

Grace paused, smiled at her then started to softly sing a song. Anna's eyelids began to close.

'Grace...' she started to say then slid into darkness.

She opened her eyes to find herself lying on the couch with one of her blankets over her, it was morning. For the first time in a long time, she had woken up without feeling the need to stifle a scream.

Sitting up she looked at Grace's painting. The harp sat alone in the sunlight. She wondered if she'd imagined Grace holding and talking to her. She didn't know what to believe. She'd think about it later, now she had to go to the auction house and start making preparations for the charity auction.

Anna saw her uncle standing in the doorway of Thompson Auctioneers as she approached the building. He stared at her for a moment, frowning, then he went inside. Her heart skipped a beat; this was not the way he normally looked at her.

Curious glances followed her as she walked into the auction house. She could feel everyone watching her. There was a note on her desk. 'Please come and see me.' It was signed by her uncle.

Nervously, she approached his office. She knew she hadn't done anything to give him any cause for concern. She was very careful around him.

'Shut the door please,' he said as she walked in.

The click sounded loud as the door locked into place.

'I don't know whether to be worried or think you've made some mistakes,' he said as she stood in front of him.

She gulped this was not sounding good.

'I contacted Mr Chisholm, who was very complimentary about your work...'

A sudden burst of white light caught Anna's attention, Grace appeared behind her uncle. Faint harp music began to play. Anna stared in fright.

'Are you listening?' her uncle said.

Anna focused back on him. There was a serious look on his face. She quickly glanced behind him, Grace was still there.

'As I was saying, Mr Chisholm was very complimentary about your work but there were some discrepancies.' He paused and gave her a considered look.

She waited, holding her breath, anxious to hear what he was going to say next.

'I'm not sure you're telling me the truth about how you are feeling just now. I phoned Sue Wilson at Rosewood Manor and asked her how you slept. She told me that you had no problems sleeping. Now I can forgive a few mistakes, but I'm beginning to wonder whether you were the right person for the job.'

Anna had to stop her hand flying to her mouth; her uncle's attitude was frightening her. With great control she stood and watched her uncle.

'Mr Chisholm said he was happy with everything you did, given how long you spent at Carlton Hall and your attention to detail.'

Her uncle paused again. 'But I'm not happy. Mr Chisholm is an important client. I have organised for a valuation assistant to go along, with the photographer, to Carlton Hall to check your work.'

She trembled in shock, the harp music got louder. She wanted to see if Grace was still behind her uncle but didn't dare look.

'Until then you will do the assistant's work, which is to list the items for the next sale. I'll speak to you again once I've decided if you're to continue working on the charity auction or not. Your health is more important to me than your involvement in the auction. I'll also talk to your aunt and we'll decide if we need to consult the doctors again.'

The harp music reached a crescendo. Her uncle picked up a piece of paper on his desk and began reading it. Anna saw Grace staring at her then she faded away along with the harp music.

Her thoughts raced as she left her uncle's office. Someone else was doing "her" job. She was the valuation specialist who normally looked after the special clients.

What was going on? Since when did a few mistakes, which she doubted she'd made, mean being taken off the charity auction.

Her uncle obviously didn't believe she was coping. She had to make him believe it. The thought of being in the doctors' clutches filled her with dread. Once they had hold of her they didn't want to let go.

Marie had typed up her notes. She'd talk to her and see if she could find out what exactly had happened

'Mr Thompson said I wasn't allowed to show you anything connected to the charity auction, Anna. I'm sorry I can't help you.'

Anna stared at Marie in amazement, not quite believing what she was hearing. *Her uncle had said that? What did he think she was going to do with the notes?*

She turned away from Marie to walk towards her desk. Her uncle was watching her from his office doorway. His gaze followed her as she walked towards her desk. She sat down and began to get on with listing the items for the next sale.

Tears of frustration threatened to creep out of her eyes. She would get a look at her notes somehow. She knew they would be kept until the assistant and photographer had returned from Carlton Hall. Her uncle kept all the information until all the details of an auction were finalised. Somehow she would find out what had happened.

She was just finishing up for the day when she saw her aunt walking into her uncle's office. It wasn't unusual to see her aunt at the auction house but her presence made Anna feel nervous. *Were they talking about her? If so, what would this mean for her?*

Laughter from Marie distracted Anna's thoughts. Recently Marie had started going out with a new boyfriend and he sometimes came to pick her up from work. He always phoned to let Marie know he was waiting for her.

'I'm just coming, John,' Marie said, a happy smile on her face. She excitedly grabbed her coat and bag and rushed out of the auction house.

Anna wanted to be able to feel that way about someone but knew she didn't dare, her heart was in too much pain.

She was checking she'd completed everything when a shadow fell across her desk. She looked straight up into the kind, smiling eyes of her aunt.

'Can you come to Paul's office please? We've something we'd like to discuss with you.'

Anna glanced around her. The few remaining members of the auction house staff were leaving quickly. Evidently they didn't want to be around to find out what was going to happen next. Her aunt hooked her arm round Anna's arm, the way she always did, and walking them to the office.

Anna's uncle gazed seriously at her as her aunt shut the office door. Anna stood facing her aunt and uncle anxious to know what they wanted to discuss with her.

'As you know,' her aunt said, 'it's coming up to the time when we all go to the concert.'

Anna's heart raced. *Was it that time already?*

'We were wondering if you'd consider staying with us the day before, so we can all travel to the concert together?' her aunt continued.

Anna couldn't breathe. White light appeared beside her. Harp music played quietly. Grace appeared beside Anna. 'I'm here, Anna, you're not alone.' Anna glanced at her.

'I told you, Jean, she's not coping,' Anna's uncle said.

'Hush, Paul,' Anna heard her aunt say, 'you're over reacting. Taking Anna off the charity auction wasn't your best decision.'

'I think I'm right, she made mistakes.'

'And you haven't?'

'Jean...'

'Quiet, Paul.'

'You don't have to stay with them, Anna,' Grace said, 'choose what you want to do.'

Anna looked at her aunt and uncle. Her aunt's welcoming smile contrasting with her uncle's concerned looking face. She didn't want to stay with them.

She was losing her ability to hold in her true feelings. She didn't know how to tell her aunt. Her uncle wouldn't believe anything she said.

'I want to stay in my flat,' she said quickly then held her breath.

Her uncle made a noise of disbelief. Her aunt gave him a gentle dig in the ribs and smiled at Anna. 'Of course, just let us know if you change your mind.'

Anna took a breath.

'Now, Paul, tell, Anna, what we agreed.'

Anna saw her aunt looking directly at her uncle. He returned the look and sighed. 'Yes, Jean.'

He turned to face Anna. 'You're back working on the charity auction.'

'And...' Anna's aunt said.

'I'm sorry I jumped to the conclusion you weren't coping.'

'Thank you,' Anna said quickly before he changed his mind.

The harp music faded away with the white light. Anna knew Grace had disappeared.

'Come round soon and see us, Anna,' her aunt said, 'I miss you.'

Anna took this as a sign that she could leave. She nodded quickly to her aunt, opened the office door and left the auction house before her aunt and uncle could stop her.

When Anna entered the lounge of her flat, Grace stepped out of a white light. Anna took one look at her and fell into darkness.

A warm man's voice was speaking when Anna opened her eyes. She was lying on her couch. Harp music was quietly playing.

'I don't think this is a good idea, Grace.'

'You're wrong, Charles. Anna needs you now. You know we've been asked to help her even if she doesn't agree she's in danger. You also know what she's about to go through and how you can help her.'

There was a moment of silence.

'She's awake, Grace,' the man said.

Anna began to push herself upright. Grace was quickly at her side and gently made her lie down again.

'You're in shock, Anna, lie still. You were so brave when you were speaking to your aunt and uncle. When you're ready I'd like to introduce you to Charles, the love of my life. He helped me when my uncle died and he can help you.'

Charles bowed his head and smiled at her. 'I'm delighted to meet you, Anna.'

Her mind was reeling, so much was happening all at once. Firstly her uncle taking her off the charity auction, then allowing her to work on it again and now Charles turning up. *Who was he? How could he help her? When would her life go back to normal?* She was scared and losing track of what was real and what wasn't. The chaos of her emotions was taking over everything. She just wanted the anniversary to be over for another year.

She began to start pushing herself up again. Grace began to gently press her down towards the couch.

'Grace...' Charles said. Grace looked at him. 'Let Anna sit up.' Grace nodded her head then removed her hand from Anna's shoulder. She went to stand beside Charles. Anna sat up.

She looked at Charles. His dark, tailored suit, with a long-tailed jacket and matching bow around a white high collared shirt matched the elegant style of Grace's dress. He smiled at her again.

'This is Charles,' Grace said gazing up at him, her eyes sparkling. She turned to Anna. 'He supported me when I needed it the most.'

'What Grace means,' he said smiling at Grace then turning to face Anna, 'is that I helped her understand what she was feeling and how to deal with it. She did all the work I just held her when she needed it.' He paused, 'Grace tells me you need the same help.'

The memory of what had happened in the auction house earlier rushed into Anna's mind. Another brick around her heart slipped out of place. She felt guilty about misleading her aunt. Her uncle was right she wasn't coping.

Could she tell her aunt the truth? A cry slipped out of her mouth and tears began to fall down her cheeks. She covered her face with her hands. The hole in the wall wasn't going to be filled in this time. More tears escaped her eyes.

Arms came round her and held her tight. She removed her hands from her face and saw, to her surprise, Charles gazing at her. 'It's okay, Anna, you can do this. You can live again.'

She remembered being in her room with her aunt holding her, after they had got home from the school, telling her everything would be okay. She had desperately wanted to believe this but knew it would never be. Her life, as she knew it, had just been destroyed.

'Anna,' Charles said pulling her out of her thoughts, 'tell me what you're thinking. I want to help you to be happy again.'

Anna stared at him for a moment. Words swam in her brain. *Could she really do it? After all the time with the doctors was it possible to say what she really was feeling?* Pain flooded her body. She cried out as hurt raced through her. Charles held her tight. She struggled to breathe.

'I've got you, Anna,' Charles said quietly, 'you're safe.'

Eventually her breathing became easier. Charles let her go, as she moved away from him, then he went to stand beside Grace.

'Charles and I will come whenever you need us,' Grace said smiling at Anna, 'let me know if you want my help with the danger I know you are in.'

Grace and Charles disappeared. Anna looked at Grace's painting and saw them walking into the garden.

She wiped her eyes as more tears threatened to fall. She didn't need anyone's help. She would get past the concert and everything would be sorted for another year. She was back working on the charity auction, which was all that mattered. Sleep claimed her quickly when her head hit her pillow.

Her aunt's smiling face slipped into her mind then she heard her uncle's voice saying he thought Anna needed more care than they could give her and her panic began.

She was standing in a hospital room watching her uncle guiding her aunt out of the room. Two hospital staff stood in front of Anna, facing her. Her uncle was telling her aunt Anna would be looked after. She tried to follow her aunt but the two hospital staff grabbed her arms and held her tight. Anna struggled, the scream began to rise in her throat...

Harp music crowded her thoughts. Charles' voice sounded loud and clear, 'You're safe Anna. It's just a dream.'

Her eyes shot open. She struggled to be released from the grip that held her tight. Charles was leaning over her bed, his hands gently but firmly holding her arms. Grace was standing behind him. Anna stared at them for a moment then lay shaking in her bed. Her breath came in short sharp bursts.

'You're safe, Anna,' Charles said again.

Anna closed her eyes, exhausted from the effort of coping with her memories. *When would it be over? Would she ever be free of her past?*

'Anna...' Charles was speaking.

Anna wearily opened her eyes.

His concerned face gazed at her. She was aware of his hands leaving her arms. 'Do you want to tell me what was happening to you?'

She shook her head to indicate she didn't. The pain would be too great.

'I'll be here when you're ready.'

Anna nodded her understanding; she knew she would never be ready. Her eyelids began to close.

'Remember, you're not alone,' she heard Charles saying.

Grace's singing was the last thing she remembered before sleep swallowed her consciousness.

Her bedroom greeted her when she opened her eyes. She stared around confused for a moment then sighed with relief. She was in her flat, her aunt and uncle wouldn't be coming to check on her. She concentrated on her breathing for a few moments steadying her nerves; she needed to be ready to face her uncle.

When Anna arrived at the auction house she eagerly started to work on the charity auction, aware of her uncle's attention on her. He had personally brought all the paperwork to her, along with the photographs of the objects from Carlton Hall. The objects were due to arrive at Thompson Auctioneers in the afternoon. He'd stared at her from his office doorway, for a few moments, before going into his office.

Relieved to be finally allowed to get on with her work Anna decided to start by looking at her written notes and what Marie had given her uncle. She was determined to discover the truth behind her 'mistakes'.

She gasped, there were no mistakes in her handwritten notes! Grace appeared before her accompanied by white light and harp music. She looked at Anna for a moment then disappeared.

Glancing at Marie, who was looking directly at her, Anna saw Marie's face turn pale, then Marie focused on her work. Anna stared at Marie in shock. *Why would Marie change her notes?*

Anna quickly got on with her work, when she noticed her uncle watching her from his office. She concentrated on pulling all the information for the charity auction guide together, determined to be the one handing the final copy to her uncle. There weren't going to be anymore 'mistakes'.

All the staff in the auction house stopped what they were doing when the Carlton Hall objects arrived. Anna listened to their comments and was particularly pleased to note that the vase was receiving the most attention. Her uncle had to be pleased that Mr Chisholm had offered her the vase.

She was admiring the Chinese dragon again when her uncle came to look at the objects with her aunt. Anna glanced nervously at them as they approached her. Her aunt gazed at the vase for several minutes then turned to Anna. 'The vase is wonderful, Anna. Congratulations on being offered it, you obviously made a great impression on Mr Chisholm.'

'Thank you,'

Anna knew her aunt took a keen interest in antiques, so any praise from her was appreciated. 'I've put the leaflet with the choice of concerts on your desk,' her aunt continued, 'let me know when you've decided what you want to hear.'

Anna nodded to her aunt she would, hoping she looked suitably excited. The concert was meant to be a happy occasion. Anna saw her uncle closely watching her.

'Come on, Paul,' her aunt said, 'let's leave Anna to get on with her work; I want to see what else is in the charity auction.'

Anna watched as her uncle allowed himself to be taken away by her aunt, squashing the panic that was threatening to show itself. She had to make everyone, in the auction house, believe everything was fine, only when she was alone in her flat would it be safe to let emotions out.

The afternoon passed quickly, with Anna checking the objects for any signs of damage and making the final adjustments to the charity auction guide. She was pleased to note the valuation assistant's report had matched hers.

She put the final copy of the auction guide on her uncle's desk for his approval before she left at the end of the day. Thankfully he wasn't in his office; Anna suspected her aunt was keeping him busy to allow Anna to get on with her work.

Even though he watched her closely at this time of year Anna knew that he loved her. During the rest of the year he always took an interest in what she was doing and didn't mind answering her questions about antiques, even if he was busy. He just wanted her to be happy.

Putting her aunt's leaflet in her bag she hoped no one noticed her hands shaking. Not long now till she was in her flat and away from prying eyes.

Marie glanced nervously at Anna as she left the auction house to meet John. She had been avoiding Anna all day which was very unlike her, normally she was happy to talk to Anna. *Why had Marie changed her notes?* This was a puzzle for another day. Anna just wanted to get home.

She started to read the leaflet as she sat on the couch, no matter how she felt about the concert she had to make a decision about what they were going to listen to, her aunt was expecting an answer.

Her mind drifted back to the first concert she'd gone to with her aunt and uncle. She had been so excited listening to the music, sitting beside them, She'd been happy. Her soul had soared with the music as it had swept over her.

Reality crashed in crowding her memories with storm clouds. Voices were telling her that she had to face the truth, the quicker she did the faster she'd be able to enjoy her life again. She had a choice to make, deal with the reality or drown in pain. She pressed her hands against her head to silence the voices, dropping the leaflet onto her knees.

Harp music flowed across her mind blowing away the black clouds and silencing the voices. Anna saw Grace and Charles step out of a circle of white light in front of her. Grace sat beside Anna and picked up the leaflet. Charles stood in front of Anna and gazed intently at her. There was a moment of silence. Anna took several deep breaths trying to calm her nerves.

'Will you tell me what you're feeling, Anna?' Charles asked.

She shook her head to indicate no, she couldn't.

'They want you to be happy and move on,' Grace said. 'Please let Charles help you.'

Anna looked at Grace in shock. *How could she know why Anna had to hide her emotions at this time every year?*

Grace nodded towards her painting. Anna turned and saw two figures standing in one of the doorways leading to the garden. She stretched out a hand towards them.

'They can only come when you're ready, Anna,' Grace said. The figures turned and walked into the garden.

'Come back, please.' Anna cried out.

'They can't, Anna.' Charles said. 'You have to be willing to let go.'

She stared at him as waves of fear washed over her. 'I can't. I... I... I won't be able to go on.'

'I know how you feel, Anna,' Grace said gently beside Anna, 'but please believe me you can do it. Charles will guide you.'

Anna looked between Grace and Charles. She knew she wanted to see the figures again but the price was too high her heart would break.

There was more silence. Anna focused on her knees, her emotions in turmoil. *Could she tell Charles how she was feeling if it meant being able to see them again?*

'I love classical music,' Grace said interrupting Anna thoughts, 'which concert do you want to listen to?' Anna looked at Grace who was reading the leaflet. Grace smiled at her, 'I like the second one.'

Anna groaned inwardly, she had completely forgotten about choosing the concert. It was all getting too much.

'It took a while for me to enjoy classical music again,' Grace said, 'but eventually I did.' Grace looked at Charles, a smile on her face. 'Charles saved me.' Charles bowed his head in thanks to Grace's comment. Grace turned to look at Anna. 'I now value the time I had with my parents.'

Anna looked at Charles. His eyes were focused on her. 'Think about it please, Anna. I can help you.'

A small part of her was beginning to listen to him, she could feel it, but the memories of talking to the doctor's still made it impossible to do.

'I'd like you to get to know my parents, Anna.' Grace said. 'Read the book.' Anna saw the *Illustrated guide to*

Rosewood Manor open on the table, with the leaflet lying on top of it.

Grace was now standing beside Charles. 'Be careful, Anna,' she said, 'the "mistakes" with your notes are only the beginning of your danger. Someone wants to harm you.'

'How do you know?' Anna stammered, feeling a chill run through her.

'Someone, who will be joining us soon, told me.' Grace said. 'If you accept my help I promise you'll never suffer at this time of year again.'

Charles and Grace walked into the white light that appeared behind them. The harp music fell silent.

Anna put the leaflet on the table and then read the book. '*Lucy and Philip Carson were both well-known musicians. They entertained music lovers, both together and apart, with their harp and violin playing. They were also accomplished singers and gave a number of recitals for royalty.*'

Anna thought about her favourite piece of classical music. It held good memories for her, yet she could only play it when she felt that she was convincing others of her ability to cope with her emotions. The memories of her watching her mum, playing the harp, and her dad, the viola, in the orchestra brought back the pain of losing them.

She looked at the book and tried to read more but gave up when her vision was obscured by silent tears running down her face. Making a decision about the concert would have to wait.

Harp music punctuated Anna's dreams that night protecting her whenever the doctor's appeared and demanded she express her emotions. She woke up exhausted.

The excitement of working on the charity auction got her to Thompson Auctioneers in the morning. She loved the fact that her job enabled her to raise funds for charity. She also knew her aunt would want to know what her choice of concert was.

Standing outside the building she took some breaths to compose herself. She had to look and act in control of her feelings to others, this was all that mattered. She'd deal with her emotions in the freedom of her flat.

The viewing of the objects for the charity auction was the next day. Anna's task for the day was to finalise all the arrangements that needed to be in place for a smooth event.

She was reading through all the replies, to the invitations to come to the viewing, when Marie approached her desk. She smiled at Marie, who took a nervous breath before speaking and looked very uncomfortable. 'Can you add John to the guest list for the viewing please, Anna?'

Anna looked at Marie surprised by her obvious discomfort; it wasn't unusual to have friends of the staff coming along to the viewings. 'Of course, I look forward to meeting him.' Marie's face paled, she nodded her thanks and hurried back to her desk.

Anna was puzzling over Marie's behaviour when a reply caught her attention; it was from Michael Caldwell, a client who Anna had known for many years. She was looking forward to finding out what he thought of the vase. She opened the reply.

'Hello Anna, I'm afraid I can't make it to the viewing, I'm not feeling very well. I'm sure it will be as successful as all the other events you have organised. Good luck and I look forward to seeing you when I am feeling better. Your friend, Michael Caldwell.'

She sat back in her seat disappointed. She had been really looking forward to talking to him. He'd always taken an interest in her career and often told her about his friends who wanted to sell their antiques.

'Anna?' a voice said beside her. Looking up she saw her uncle standing by her desk. His face was one of concern.

'Michael Caldwell can't come to the viewing he's not well. I was looking forward to showing him the vase.'

Her uncle nodded his understanding. 'I'll make sure an auction guide is sent to him. The guide is wonderful; you've certainly done an excellent job. I'm sure we'll have lots of interested buyers at the auction.'

Anna stared at him in surprise then hurriedly replied to him, 'Thank you.' She wondered what was behind his change of behaviour.

'Your aunt has asked me to find out which concert you want to go to.'

Anna took a quick breath, she realised that she'd forgotten to choose a concert to go to. 'The second one please,' she said quickly, remembering this was the one Grace had pointed out. 'I'm afraid I've left the leaflet at home. I'll have to bring it in tomorrow.'

'That's no problem, Anna, your aunt has her own copy of the leaflet, I'll let her know.'

Anna watched him walk back to his office not quite sure what to make of what had just happened. She heard his voice coming out of the office. 'The second concert, Jean, and yes I was encouraging when I spoke to her.' There was a pause, then he spoke again. 'I know you're right and I'm over reacting, just as you said.'

Anna quickly got her head down and looked at the other replies on her desk, her mind racing. Her aunt clearly believed she was coping. Terror gripped Anna's stomach. *What would her aunt say if she knew the truth?*

Anna was aware of harp music playing and white light at the edge of her vision. She didn't dare look up, she knew she'd see Grace and be reminded that her control of her emotions was fragile.

She stared at her desk until one of the auction staff came and asked her a question. The rest of the day flew by with Anna deliberately only thinking about the charity auction, anything else threatened to unravel her.

Marie speaking, after a phone rang, let Anna know it was the end of the day. 'Hi John, yes I'm ready. I'll be right out.' There was a short pause, 'Yes, I got you an invitation.'

Anna looked at Marie expecting to see a happy smile on her face. Marie gazed unhappily at Anna then rushed out of the building. Anna stared in amazement after Marie. *What was going on with her?* She was still thinking about this when she walked into her lounge.

'Why is Marie acting like that, Anna? That's the question you have to ask yourself,' Grace said.

Anna jumped and saw Grace standing beside the harp in her painting looking into the lounge. Charles stood beside Grace. He bowed to Anna then spoke, 'How would your aunt feel if she knew the truth?'

Anna stared at the painting in shock. *How did Charles know about her aunt? What did Grace mean by her question?*

Grace and Charles stepped out of white light into the lounge, harp music began to play. Anna backed away from them as they approached her. The wall behind her stopped her progress. Grace and Charles stood together facing her, both looking very serious.

'How do you know about my aunt?' she said staring at Charles.

'Grace told me about your uncle's phone call to your aunt today.'

'How do you know about the phone call? Anna said staring at Grace in shock.

'I tell Charles everything that goes on in the auction house, Anna; he needs to know so he can help you.'

Anna's hands grabbed the walls as she began to feel light-headed. Charles was swiftly at her side holding her up.

'But you only appear for a moment, Grace,' Anna managed to say faintly before her world really started spinning.

She was sitting on the couch when her head became steady again. Grace was sitting beside her and Charles was standing facing her, clearly watching her.

'I'm always in the auction house, Anna,' Grace said. 'I don't always show myself to you. I need to know where your danger is coming from.'

Anna looked at Grace. 'Why?' Anna managed to say after a few moments.

'Because someone wants to use your pain to gain something that isn't theirs. I also know what you're going through and want to heal your heart so you can live again.'

Anna suddenly heard her uncle again, speaking to her aunt saying he was agreeing that Anna was coping. She gasped as a number of bricks slid out of the wall around her heart. Tears silently flood down her cheeks. She clutched her arms around her middle.

'Anna,' Charles said. She focused on him. 'Please tell me what you're feeling.' She shook her head indicating she couldn't. The harp music got a little louder.

'They want to know,' he said then pointed to the painting.

Anna wiped her eyes and looked at the picture. Two figures, with encouraging smiles on their faces, now stood beside the harp facing into the lounge. Anna's heart leapt at the sight of the figures and remembered her childhood memories as she breathed in. 'You can do it, I promise,' one of the figures said, 'trust Charles.'

Anna turned to face Charles. She had to do it; she just didn't know how she was going to deal with the pain.

He smiled gently at her. 'I'd like to start when you were told the news. Where were you?'

Anna took some deep breaths then spoke quietly. 'At the school concert, I'd just finished singing on stage with the group.'

The memory of the excitement of performing followed by the crash of shock threatened to overwhelm her. She felt Grace hold her hand as tears filled her eyes.

'You can do this,' Grace said quietly beside her.

Anna blinked then wiped her eyes with her free hand.

'What happened next?' Charles said.

Anna had to pause, the pain threatened to drown her ability to speak. Grace gently squeezed her hand. Anna looked at Charles. 'I... I was taken to a room where my aunt and uncle were waiting for me and my teacher was there. My uncle told me...' Anna let out a sob. Grace's arms came around her and held her tight.

Anna was back in the room with the understanding looks and her aunt holding her. It wasn't fair. Why did it have to happen to her? She got home somehow. She didn't remember how. Home where her parents would never be returning to, the car crash had ended her happy home forever. Then there was a period of time she lost. Gentle harp music surrounded her.

'Anna,' this was Charles pulling her from her thoughts. She gazed at him her mind in the depths of emptiness. 'You're doing really well,' he said. 'What happened next?'

'I was being looked after by my aunt and uncle until...' *The doctor's* she thought unable to say it. This period of her life was worse than when she'd been told the news.

'Anna...' Charles gently prompted her.

'I can't,' she said, 'please don't ask me.'

'You can do it,' the figure from the painting said, 'I believe in you.'

Anna took a deep breath, 'The doctors,' she said in a rush. Then she burst into floods of tears, the pain overpowering any other thoughts in her head. Her only awareness was Grace's arms around her.

The voice of the figure in the painting drifted into Anna's consciousness as her tears came to an end. 'Well done, remember, you're always in our thoughts.'

She looked at the painting. The two figures were walking through the doors into the garden.

'Well done,' said Grace. Anna turned to see Grace smiling at her. 'The first step is the hardest; it does get easier I promise.' Grace let Anna go and then went to stand beside Charles. Anna braced herself for more questions from Charles as she expected him to treat her as the doctor's had.

'We'll go now, Anna,' he said, 'you've taken the most important step, the next one's are easier.'

They turned and walked into the white light behind them, the harp music faded away as the white light disappeared. Anna looked again at the painting hoping to see the two figures. The harp stood alone in the room.

Her heart ached as the pain flowed out of the gaps in the walls around her heart, there was nothing she could do to stop it happening. After the concert she'd build the walls back-up again, stronger than before, she could do that. She didn't believe she was in any danger as Grace claimed either.

She thought about Grace's question about Marie again. Anna knew that whatever was happening with Marie was totally unrelated to the anniversary. She was going to concentrate on making the charity auction as successful as possible, this way she'd prove that she could control her emotions and work at the auction house. Her aunt and uncle would leave her alone and her life would go back to normal.

She woke up the next morning tired and emotionally drained having battled the doctor's voices as they tried to pull her back into their clutches. Several times she had been aware of harp music and thought she could feel hands on her shoulders. The figures from the painting had appeared in her dreams too. Everything was a jumble of thoughts. She took one last look at the painting as she left her flat; the harp was alone in the room.

Anna looked around the viewing room in Thompson Auctioneers, where the objects for the auction were on display, and shivered, remembering that Grace had said she was always in the auction house. The thought that someone was always watching her scared her. She spotted Marie coming into the room with a man and went to greet them. A successful viewing was important before a sale.

Marie glanced nervously at the man before smiling at Anna. The man looked directly at Anna and offered his hand to her. His face lit up with an engaging smile. 'Hello, Anna, I'm John. I'm very pleased to meet you. Marie has told me so many wonderful things about you.'

Anna paused for a moment, taken aback by the warmth of his greeting; she was reminded of Charles and his confident, self-assured bearing. She could see why Marie was going out with him. She glanced at Marie who quickly rearranged her anxious face into another smile.

'It's lovely to meet you, John, welcome to Thompson Auctioneers.'

'Thank you, I'm looking forward to examining all the objects in the charity auction. I believe there's a very special vase I must see.'

Anna smiled at him, pleased Marie had told him about the vase. The more people who knew about it, the better the chances of raising an excellent sale price.

'Yes, I was very honoured to be offered the vase for the auction.'

'I'm sure you deserved the offer, Marie tells me you are very thorough in your work.'

Anna glanced at Marie again. A nervous smile crossed Marie's face.

'We'll let you get on with your work, Anna,' John said, 'I look forward to coming to the sale. I'm sure I'll see something I want to buy today.'

She watched them walk round the room, thinking he looked vaguely familiar but wasn't sure why. John had his arm on Marie's back gently guiding her through the crowd. His dark blue jacket and trousers and open-necked white shirt complemented the easygoing and amicable manner he clearly had. She was reminded of Charles and how he treated Grace.

'There you are,' Anna's aunt said breaking into Anna's thoughts. Anna turned to see her aunt and uncle entering the room. Her aunt gave her a hug.

'This is wonderful,' her aunt said. 'You've surpassed yourself this time; there are so many people here.'

Anna beamed at her aunt. 'Thank you, I appreciate your confidence. I just want the auction to go well.'

'I know it will,' her uncle said, 'I have every confidence in your ability to select interesting items.' Anna smiled at him pleased that at last he seemed to be happy with her.

'I just have to look at that amazing vase again,' her aunt said smiling at Anna. Anna looked at where the vase was, Marie and John were amongst the crowd gazing at it and talking excitedly.

'I've booked the concert tickets,' her aunt said. 'Your choice of concert was excellent.'

Anna watched her aunt and uncle walk away from her, a chill running through her, the concert choice was Grace's not Anna's. She wondered where Grace was and had she heard her aunt's comment. She didn't have time to think about this anymore as more people were coming into the room.

The viewing went quickly and before Anna knew it the room was beginning to empty. The noise level had dropped from loud, excited chatter to quiet conversation. John was taking another look at the vase and Anna had noticed that he had been around the whole room. She hoped this meant he would be at the sale buying something.

Her thoughts drifted to Michael Caldwell. She hoped she would see him soon. He'd turned from a client into a friend and he had said he viewed her as his daughter in the past.

A voice brought her back to the room. 'I have a special book I'd like to donate to the sale, if I may, Mr Thompson,' this was John.

'Please call me, Paul,' her uncle said. 'I'd be delighted to accept your book, thank you very much.' She looked at John and her uncle standing by the door to the room. Marie was standing patiently by John and her aunt was by her uncle, smiling. John smiled and nodded in Anna's direction when he saw her looking at him.

'I'll give the book to Marie tomorrow, Anna. I'm sure you'll find it interesting.' She nodded her thanks and understanding. John took Marie out of the room, his arm firmly round her body. Anna heard him speaking, 'Thank you for an interesting viewing, Marie, I've learned so much.' Marie's hesitant reply was lost as she and John walked away from the room.

Soon only Anna and her aunt and uncle were left in the room.

'Well done,' her uncle said as they walked out of the room. Anna took a last look into the room and locked the door behind her.

'Thank you,' she said looking at him.

'We're going out for dinner to celebrate the success of the viewing,' her aunt said. 'Would you like to join us?'

Anna nodded she would. She was in a relaxed mood. The viewing had gone well and her aunt and uncle believed she was coping, life was good.

She watched her aunt and uncle drive away as she stood outside the building where her flat was. The evening had been wonderful, just like the rest of the year. She was happy.

Grace and Charles walked through white light, accompanied by harp music, as Anna entered her lounge. The door shut with a firm click behind her. Anna jumped in fright.

'I'm pleased your aunt likes my choice of concert,' Grace said, 'I know you'll enjoy it.'

'You were there all the time? 'Anna stammered looking at Grace.

'Yes I was.'

Anna was about to ask why, as she was happy and her aunt and uncle believed she was coping when Charles spoke, 'It's time, Anna, you have to take the next step.'

Anna stepped back towards the door. Her hand pressed down on the handle. It didn't move.

'No,' she said looking at Charles. 'Everything's okay, my aunt and uncle believe I'm coping, the viewing went well, there's no danger.'

'There was,' Grace said, 'you just didn't know it.'

'You didn't show yourself,' Anna said, 'you must be wrong.'

'You needed to be yourself,' Grace said, 'I'll tell you more if you accept my help.'

'I don't need your help, leave me alone.'

Anna rattled the door handle again. The door stayed firmly shut.

She stared furiously at Grace and Charles. She was about to demand they let her go when the voice of the figure in the painting spoke. 'We can't come any closer, Anna. There must be more for you to deal with.'

Anna stared at the painting. The two figures were standing in front of the harp looking directly at her, gentle smiles on their faces. Familiar perfume comforted her. 'Did you ask Charles and Grace to help me?' Anna said remembering hearing Grace telling Charles someone had asked them to help her.

'Yes,' the figure said. 'We've been watching over you. When we realised Grace had contacted you we asked her and Charles for their help. Grace told us about the danger you're in too. We hoped if you accepted Grace's help, with your danger, you'd let her and Charles heal your heart. As you weren't accepting Grace's help we decided to ask Charles and Grace to help you anyway. You have to deal with the pain to fully live your life; this is all we want for you. If you don't you'll miss out on the happiness we know you deserve. We'll always be watching over you. Please accept Grace's offer of help with your danger, it's very real.'

Anna's hand fell away from the door handle and wiped away the tear that had rolled down her face, as the harp music flowed around her. Silence filled her lounge. She shut her eyes to avoid seeing Charles, Grace and the two figures watching her. Around her heart the final pieces of the walls fell away. She knew that she could never rebuild them. She was destined to feel the pain forever more. She couldn't carry on with the charity auction any more. Her life had fallen apart.

'Anna,' Charles said stopping her thoughts. She opened her eyes, only then becoming aware of the silent tears streaming down her face. She let them fall. He gave her encouraging smile. 'What happened after the doctors?'

Anna glanced at the painting then back to Charles. *In her mind she was in the hospital room again except this time her uncle was coming in and demanding that Anna be allowed to come home. Home, Anna thought, and living with her aunt and uncle had become home.*

Her aunt had followed her uncle into the room and rushed up to Anna wrapping her arms around her. Her aunt's reports of her visits to Anna had convinced her uncle that Anna needed to be home instead of in the hospital.

Anna focused on the painting. 'My aunt and uncle came to the hospital and took me to live with them.' She paused then took a deep breath, 'I managed to convince them I was coping but,' she paused again, 'really I was pretending. I hid my pain. I didn't want to let you go. I didn't want to forget you.'

The two figures smiled at Anna. There was silence in the room. Anna looked at Charles and Grace who smiled at her.

'Well done,' Charles said.

Grace came to Anna's side and led her to the couch, sitting her down. Anna looked at her. 'Can I see them now?' Anna asked.

'Not just yet, Anna, you need to rest. They'll come to you soon I promise.'

Anna heard the harp music getting louder, waves of sleepiness swept over her. 'I want to see them now,' she said as her eyes closed.

'Give yourself time to heal,' Charles said. 'I promise you'll see them soon.' Darkness descended over her.

Someone was shaking her awake. She opened her eyes to see Grace leaning over her as she lay on the couch. She felt different somehow, more settled inside. Whatever had happened as she had slept had definitely helped how she was feeling. She tried to look at the painting.

'Get up quickly,' Grace said. Anna heard her flat door open.

'Grace!' Anna heard Charles said urgently. He was standing by Anna's bedroom door.

'Hurry,' Grace said pulling Anna up and pushing her towards Charles.

Anna found herself bundled into her bedroom with Charles and Grace following her. Charles shut the door quietly.

'What...?' Anna said. Grace motioned for Anna to be quiet. Grace's painting was on her bedroom wall. She remembered the Rosewood Manor book was on the table. The sound of the lounge door opening stopped her from going back into the lounge. She knew she had the only set of keys for her flat. Charles stood by the door listening. Grace stood by Anna her hand firmly on Anna's arm.

Charles stepped back as the bedroom door opened. Anna stifled a gasp as a man she had never seen before, dressed in a dark jacket and trousers, looked into the room.

'Is she there?' a voice said.

'No, there's no one here.'

'Pity, I was looking forward to giving her a scare and reminding her how stressful this time of year was for her. Marie was an excellent source of information. The description of how Anna reacts to the mention of her parents was very useful to John.'

The first man walked back into the lounge leaving the door open. Anna saw a second man, dressed just like the first, go around her lounge turning over her furniture and scattering her belongings around the room. The first man picked the Rosewood Manor book off the table before the second one turn the table over.

'You got it?' the second man said.

'Yes,' the first said, 'she'll never know we've taken it. Come on let's go.'

Anna listened as the front door shut. She began to shake violently. Grace gently sat her down onto the bed. Charles went into the lounge. He returned a moment later. 'They've gone.'

Anna got slowly to her feet and walked into her lounge. A cry of shock came out of her mouth as she surveyed the scene. The phone rang. Charles search through the destruction for the phone. Anna answered it. 'Yes.'

'Anna, please come to the auction house immediately,' her uncle said.

She stared at the phone as the dialling tone sounded on the other end of the phone line.

'Do you want my help, Anna?' Grace said.

Anna stared at Grace unable to take everything in that was happening.

'Just nod if you do,' Grace said.

Anna nodded she did.

'Go to the auction house. Charles and I will look after you,' Grace said.

Anna approached Thompson Auctioneers feeling like she was in a bad dream. Charles and Grace had helped her find her bag and told her to act normally. *What was that after having her flat being broken into? How had the two men had known where she'd lived?*

Her aunt and uncle knew her address but would never have had someone break into her flat. Everyone at the auction house knew the personal details kept there were not to be shared.

Police cars in front of the auction house made Anna jump. *What was going on?*

In the auction house the door to the viewing room was open with police going in and out. On her desk sat an envelope with a note on top of it. She read the note,

> *'Here is the book as promised. I hope it raises a lot of money. John Caldwell.'*

Opening the envelope she read the title of the book *Rosewood Manor - An Illustrated History*. Anna grabbed at the edge of her desk. Her uncle's voice called out her name. She looked towards his office.

'Please can you come here, Anna.'

She walked to his office and saw two other men when she entered. One was Michael Caldwell's chauffeur, wearing his smart, light grey uniform with matching hat, who had driven Anna many times before. The other was an older man with dark, short hair, wearing a tailored navy suit, he gazed intently at her.

All three men stared at her for a moment. The man wearing the navy suit turned to the chauffeur, 'If you're absolutely certain this can't wait.'

'My instructions are very clear, Inspector Taylor, as I told you.'

The Inspector frowned then glanced at her, 'Please come straight back, Miss Thompson.'

Anna nodded she would in a daze. She had no idea where she was going let alone why she had to come straight back to the auction house.

Thoughts raced through Anna's head as the chauffeur drove her to her destination. *Why was all this happening to her? Who was behind the break-in? How had John Caldwell got the book stolen from her flat? Where did Marie fit in with everything? The book had to have been given to her uncle by Marie and John had said he'd give the book to Marie for the auction.* She was so confused. Michael had never mentioned having a son and Anna had never seen any pictures of any children in all the times she had been to his house.

She closed her eyes trying to shut out everything that was happening to her. The car stopped. Opening her eyes she saw the front of Michael's house. She breathed a sigh of relief, Michael would tell her who John was she was sure of this.

Michael's study door was opened by a man she didn't recognise. He was wearing a dark suit with a white shirt and black tie. His hair had streaks of silver through it. He had a serious look on his face.

'Miss Thompson, please take a seat and then we can begin.'

'Where's Michael?'

'I'll explain everything in a moment, please be seated.'

Uncertainly Anna began to walk to the dark, polished wood chair, which was positioned in front of the large decorative mahogany desk. A sudden noise and shouting made her turn round. 'I demand to be included.'

Footsteps pounding up the stairs she had just climbed to get to the study. John appeared in the study doorway and tried to push past the man who'd greeted Anna.

'Mr Caldwell, you know you can't be here, only the beneficiaries to the Will are allowed. You are not a beneficiary, as you are well aware.'

Anna's heart skipped a beat. He had said Will and there was no one else in the room. That meant someone was dead. The room started to sway. A hand caught her arm and held her steady. Anna heard harp music and turned to see Grace, surrounded by white light, beside her. 'I've got you,' Grace said.

'I'm going,' John said as the chauffeur appeared beside him and grabbed his arm firmly. 'I'll get what's mine, Anna, just you wait and see,' John said as the chauffeur dragged him away.

Anna was aware of the man closing the study door then everything disappeared.

She was looking up into the man's face when she opened her eyes. Arms gently slid beneath her shoulders and began to sit her up. Anna turned to see the chauffeur beside her.

'I'm so sorry you had to see that, Miss Thompson,' the man said as he and the chauffeur guided her to the chair. 'John knew his father's wishes. I don't know why he came here today.'

Once Anna was safely in the chair the man sat down, behind the desk, facing Anna, the chauffeur left the study. The man picked up some sheets of paper then focused on her. My name is Mr Thornton, Miss Thompson. I am the executor of Michael Caldwell's estate and have been instructed to read to you, as the sole beneficiary of his Will, the following...'

Anna clutched the envelope in her hands as the chauffeur drove her away from "her" home. Mr Thornton had handed her the envelope and told her it was imperative that she followed the instructions in every detail, starting with reading the contents of the letter the moment she got into the car.

Her mind was numb, Michael was dead, John was his son and she had inherited everything. She couldn't begin to think about reading the contents of the envelope just now.

'Please open the envelope, Miss Thompson,' the chauffeur said bringing her back to her reality, 'Mr Caldwell was most insistent that you do that.'

Reluctantly Anna began to open the envelope with shaking hands. Two letters were inside. Anna recognised Michael's handwriting and began to cry.

'Please, Miss Thompson,' the chauffeur said, 'you must read the contents; Mr Caldwell stressed how important this was to me.'

Anna wiped her eyes and looked at the letters, one was marked 'To the police, to be opened immediately', the other was addressed to her.

She opened the one addressed to her. She took a deep breath then began to read it.

'Dearest Anna, I wish I could speak to you in person but this unfortunately won't be happening. My health is failing faster than I expected. I want you to inherit my estate as I know you will value and look after my collections. I have a son I've never told you about but must now as I am aware that he is back in the country after hearing of my ill health. His name is John and he is very dangerous. Please be careful if you meet him, he will try to hurt you.'

Anna closed her eyes she couldn't read anymore, images of her flat and the book flashed into her mind.

'Miss Thompson, please keep reading,' the chauffeur said, 'I can only keep driving for so long before the police come looking for me. Mr Caldwell needs you to do as he asks.'

She opened her eyes and continued to read.

'I discovered many years ago that John was selling stolen antiques claiming he owned them. I disinherited him, something he didn't like. He quickly left the country before the police could arrest him. The second letter must be given to the police immediately.

John will do anything to discredit you. If you are suspected of being involved in any activity that requires police attention John can challenge my Will. The second letter will stop John from making any challenges. Remember, I love you as a daughter. Live a happy life, Anna. Michael Caldwell.'

More tears filled her eyes.

'I have to head to the auction house now, Miss Thompson,' the chauffeur said. 'Are you ready?'

She shook her head the last place she wanted to be was at the auction house. She was feeling too fragile. Her uncle would take one look at her and assume she wasn't coping no matter what her aunt said. Too much had happened too quickly to her.

'I could delay getting to the auction house if you had to go somewhere first,' the chauffeur suggested.

'Come to the flat,' Anna heard Grace saying.

'Can we go to my flat, please?.'

'Of course, what's the address?'

Anna opened the flat door; the chauffeur was waiting in the car. He said he'd wait for 10 minutes then come and find her to take her to the auction house. The first thing she saw when she walked into her lounge was the blue Chinese dragon vase sitting on the floor. She simply stared at it in shock. Grace and Charles appeared before her in white light, along with the harp music.

Grace came straight to her side. 'Listen to me, Anna,' she said urgently. 'Give the police the letter from Michael Caldwell. Charles and I will make sure the vase is found in the house of the person who put it in your flat.' She paused them continued, 'Do you understand?'

Anna watched Charles carefully lift the vase up then she focused on Grace.

'Nod if you understand, there isn't much time,' Grace said.

Anna nodded she did and continued to look at Grace. 'The letter,' Grace said again. Anna took the letter out of the envelope and held it in her hand. Grace joined Charles in the white light.

'I opened your front door,' Grace said as the light disappeared and the music faded away. 'The police are coming, remember what I said.'

Footsteps and voices came towards the lounge. A police woman and the chauffeur rushed in. Anna held out the letter towards the police woman then the world began to spin. The chauffeur caught her as her legs gave way; the letter fell out of her fingers.

Voices brought her back to consciousness. She was lying on her bed with the chauffeur standing by her side. The police woman was standing in the doorway talking on the radio. In the lounge other police officers were searching through her belongings.

'Yes, Inspector,' 'the police woman said, 'that's what the chauffeur said. 'John tried to crash the Will reading, even though he wasn't a beneficiary, and he is named in the letter Miss Thompson was holding.'

The police woman looked at Anna. 'She's awake. She looks very pale. What do you want me to do?' There was a moment of silence. The radio burst into life. 'Please bring Miss Thompson to the auction house as soon as she feels able.'

'Yes, Sir,' the policewoman said then looked at Anna.

'Miss Thompson,' the chauffeur said, 'would you like me to accompany you?'

Anna closed her eyes for a moment and gathered what little strength she had left. She had to trust Grace and Charles would help her and that everything would be okay. She didn't think much else could happen to her today. Opening her eyes she nodded to the chauffeur that she wanted him to accompany her. Grace's painting was still on her bedroom wall.

As she walked through the mess in the lounge she wondered if her flat would ever feel safe again. Living with her aunt and uncle was very appealing at the moment. The chauffeur insisted on driving her to the auction house, the policewoman tried to argue but he said it was his duty as he was now Anna's chauffeur.

Anna sat in the back of Michael Caldwell's car until the matter was settled; she just wanted the day to be over. She shut her eyes and let the voices outside the car wash over her. A door opening and closing made her open her eyes; the chauffeur was sitting in the driver's seat. 'I won't leave you, Miss Thompson, of that you can be assured,' he said looking at her. Anna nodded her thanks then closed her eyes again.

Too soon the car stopped. Anna knew they had to be at the auction house. Her nightmare day just kept on going. Taking a deep breath she opened her eyes. The chauffeur was watching her in the top mirror. 'I'll be by your side, Miss Thompson, no one will harm you.' Anna nodded her thanks and hoped he was right.

Everyone looked at her as she entered the auction house. Around the room amongst the numerous police officers were her aunt and uncle, the auction house staff including Marie. John was standing beside Marie. Anna jumped; the chauffeur positioned himself so he was between Anna and John. John had a triumphant look on his face. Inspector Taylor was standing in the middle of the room watching her.

'Thank you for coming, Miss Thompson,' he said. 'I realise you've already been through a lot today. I'll make this as quick as I can. Please will you sit in the chair beside your desk.' Anna sat down gratefully; she didn't think her legs would have held her up much longer.

Anna saw Inspector Taylor take Michael Caldwell's letter from the police woman and read it. No one said a word. He folded her letter, put it in his pocket, then swept his gaze over everyone in the room.

'We're all here today because last night a valuable vase was stolen.'

Anna cried in shock, remembering seeing the vase in her lounge. If the police had found it John would have had grounds to contest Michael's will. She wondered where Grace and Charles had taken it.

Inspector Taylor turned to her, 'I'm sorry to give you more distressing news, Miss Thompson. There are police teams searching for the vase right now. I know you were the one who secured the vase for the charity auction. As soon as I know where it is I'll tell you.'

Anna glanced around the room; her aunt was staring at her obviously distressed by Anna's appearance. John was watching her closely. Anna shivered in fear. *What was he going to do when he discovered the vase wasn't found in her flat?* The chauffeur moved a little closer to her.

Inspector Taylor nodded his head to the police woman who'd been in Anna's flat. The police woman walked from where she was to stand the other side of Anna from the chauffeur.

He continued speaking, 'The viewing room was locked by Miss Thompson, witnessed by Mr and Mrs Thompson. I am certain Miss Thompson had nothing to do with the theft, given the fact that she had secured the vase to sell at the charity auction. Her flat is being searched as are all your homes. Mr Caldwell is the exception as he is here supporting Marie. I will be talking to him later as I know he attended the viewing.'

Anna thought of the mess her flat was in after the break-in, a tear trickled down her face, all she'd wanted was a home of our own where she could be happy. The chauffeur handed her a handkerchief. She gave him a small smile and dried her face.

'I would like to thank John Caldwell for coming to support Marie after she requested his assistance,' Inspector Taylor said.

Anna looked at Marie who was standing beside John. Marie was glancing nervously at John, holding her hands tightly against her legs. John smiled and put his arm around Marie, who flinched.

'I appreciate everyone's cooperation in this matter,' Inspector Taylor said. Silence filled the room then he continued, 'Whilst I'm waiting for the teams to report there's one matter I'd like to discuss.'

Anna saw him pick up a book of the nearest desk to him and recognised it immediately; it was *Rosewood Manor - An Illustrated History*.

White light appeared in front of Anna. Harp music began to play quietly. Charles and Grace stepped into the room. Anna cried out in shock. Charles nodded his head to Anna and made his way to stand by the door to the room. Grace stood just in front of Anna and smiled at her. Inspector Taylor glanced at Anna, a frown on his face.

'Are you okay, Miss Thompson? Do you need to see a doctor?'

Anna jumped in fright; a doctor was the last person she wanted to see at this moment. She shook her head to indicate she didn't want to see a doctor.

'I'll let you go as soon as I can,' Inspector Taylor said.

Anna nodded her understanding. She saw the grin that had appeared on John's face fade. Inspector Taylor turned to face John.

'Charles and I are here for you,' Grace said leaning towards Anna. 'We won't let anything happen to you.

'Mr Caldwell,' Inspector Taylor said, ' I noticed Miss Thompson's unusual reaction to this book and the note that came with it. Could you tell me please where you got it from?'

The harp music got a little louder. John smiled at the Inspector.

'Of course, Inspector. It's been in the family for many years, my father...'

'If you'll excuse me one moment Mr Caldwell,' Inspector Taylor said as a police officer approached him with a note. He gave the book to the police officer then stared intently at the note. He looked at Anna then John. Anna began to tremble, something bad was about to happen she just knew it.

'Not long now, Anna,' Grace said.

The harp music changed, it flowed over Anna calming her nerves. Inspector Taylor focused on Anna. 'Nothing was found at your flat, Miss Thompson.'

A look of shock crossed John's face.

'I will have someone come round and talk to you about your break-in after everything is completed here.'

Anna saw her aunt gasp in shock.

'I'd suggest staying somewhere else for the moment,' Inspector Taylor continued, 'until you've had time to clear up the mess.'

'Miss Thompson will be at Mr Michael Caldwell's house, Inspector,' Anna heard the chauffeur saying before she could answer.

Anna looked at her aunt and uncle; she could see her aunt really wanted Anna to stay with them.

'Thank you,' Inspector Taylor said nodding to the chauffeur.

'You'll be well looked after, Anna,' Grace said.

Anna nodded absentmindedly, no one in Michael's house would let John harm her she knew it. She relaxed a little, letting her thoughts drift away from the room.

'Now, Mr Caldwell,' Inspector Taylor said. 'I have to inform you that your house will now be searched. I contacted Rosewood Manor after Miss Thompson left the auction house earlier, after seeing her reaction to the book on her desk. Sue Wilson informed me she had leant the book, you claimed to be yours, to Miss Thompson. I've also been told you paid close attention to the vase in the viewing and I have information which suggests you are a person of interest in this theft. Please can you tell me where you were between leaving the viewing and coming to the auction house to support Marie.'

Anna was vaguely aware of John saying something to the Inspector. Harp music was in the background to her thoughts.

'Think, Anna. Who knew your flat address?' she heard Grace saying.

Anna looked at Grace puzzled. *What was she supposed to be remembering?* She looked at John; his face was a mask of barely controlled anger. Then it hit her.

'You were at Rosewood Manor,' she said abruptly standing up and pointing her finger at John. 'That's where I wrote my address in the guest comment's book.'

John snarled then launched himself at her. Grace grabbed Anna's arm as people started screaming, Marie, her aunt and possibly herself. Hands tried to grab her. A voice called out, 'get him.'

'This way,' Grace said.

Anna followed Grace through the mass of moving bodies. The harp music drowning out the noises of chaos around her.

'Grace,' Anna heard Charles saying.

Charles was standing in white light by the door, his hand stretched out towards her and Grace. Behind her voices called out her name. As she reached the doorway Charles took hold of her other arm and then there was only the harp music.

Anna looked around not recognising where she was for a moment and who was playing the music. It sounded like Grace's harp was being played but Grace and Charles were standing in front of her.

'Behind you, Anna,' Grace said smiling at her.

Anna turned around puzzled. Sitting playing the harp, in the room beside the gardens, was one of the figures, she had last seen alive, when her aunt and uncle had come to collect her to take her to the school show before the accident. The other figure was standing beside the harp beaming at her.

'Dad! Mum!'

She flung herself at her dad who caught her as her mum lifted her fingers off the harp strings. The sound gently faded away to nothing. Anna's heart soared. Tears tumbled from her eyes. Her dad held her until they stopped. He gently let go of her and moved aside to allow Anna's mum to take his place. Anna breathed in the comforting smell of her mum's perfume. She didn't want to let go off the love and security she'd lost all those years ago. Eventually her mum let Anna go.

Anna stared at her not wanting the moment to end. Now she had her mum and dad back she wanted to stay with them forever.

' There's someone else here who'd like to say hello, Anna,' Charles said breaking her concentration.

'You won't disappear will you if I turn round.' Anna asked her mum.

Her mum laughed gently, 'No I won't.'

Anna reluctantly turned round to Charles and saw Michael Caldwell coming into the room from the garden. He smiled at her.

'Thank you, Anna, for your bravery. You've helped me bring John to the police's attention. The letter you gave the police detailed all John's crimes that I knew about. I wish you a long and happy life and look forward to seeing what you add to my collections.' He stepped forward and gave her a hug. Then he went into the garden.

She turned back to her parents and knew that the pain she'd carried around for all those years was gone. She turned to look at Charles and Grace, 'Thank you, I owe you so much.'

'You did all the work, Anna,' Charles said, 'We just guided you.'

Grace stepped forward and wrapped her arms around Anna. 'I enjoyed helping you. It was worth it to see you hugging your parents. I know you'll be happy from now on. Come to Rosewood Manor if you want to speak to me.'

'The book,' Anna said suddenly remembering it was at the auction house.

'Will be returned when the police are finished with it,' Grace said. 'Everyone in the auction house thinks you ran out of the building. They'll come to your flat soon to see if you are there. 'It's time to say goodbye.'

'Please no,' Anna said as she saw her parents walking behind Charles and Grace, 'take me with you.' Anna thought her heart was going to break all over again.

'You can't come with us, Anna,' her mum said, 'you have your whole life to live.'

Grace and Charles moved aside to let Anna's mum and dad through to stand before Anna. Anna was surrounded by her parents' love for one last time.

'Remember, we'll always be watching over you,' her dad said. 'Enjoy your life. One day we will meet again.'

'Enjoy the concert, and remember, we always played for you when we were in the orchestra,' her mum said.

Charles smiled and bowed to Anna then followed Anna's parents into the garden. At the light touch of Grace's hand Anna found herself standing in her lounge looking at a smiling Grace, who was in the painting, which was hanging on the wall.

'Goodbye, Anna,' Grace said then she joined the others in the garden.

Anna watched as they all smiled at her then turned and walked away into the garden. The painting began to disappear.

Banging noises came from her front door, voices called out her name. Her aunt, uncle, the chauffeur and Inspector Taylor burst into the lounge. Her aunt wrapped unconditional love around Anna.

'My Mum... Dad... they're really gone,' Anna managed to say just before tears filled her eyes.

Her uncle's arms came round the other side of Anna. 'Let us look after you, Anna,' he said. 'We love you.'

PASSENGER 82

LYNDSAY KELLY

Passenger 82

Sitting in the dark with her knees pulled against her chest, she held her breath, trying not to make a sound. She could hear the footsteps as they moved around, and she strained to hear where they were coming from. She knew this day would come. With every noise, she hugged her knees tighter, feeling like her body might explode. There was no way of escaping, she knew that sooner or later the door to the small cupboard would open. There was no way out. They had found her.

'Greta...' sang the voice of a man. 'Greta, we know you're here.'

A tear fell from her eye down her face as the pain in her chest grew. The footsteps were moving closer now and with a thump, someone stopped in front of her hiding place.

She closed her eyes, waiting for the hands to grab her as the cupboard door swung open.

THUD.

Maggie jumped from her bed, looking around the small room, looking for someone in the dark, but she was alone. Her uniform for work hung neatly on the wardrobe door, a reminder that she was no longer that child.

'Just a dream.' She sighed, knowing she would not get any more sleep now.

*

Standing on the tarmac, Maggie looked up at the new aircraft, the silver fuselage glinting in the light. Beyond the runway, she could see dark clouds, bringing a storm towards her. She had tried to shake the fear the dream had evoked, telling herself there was nothing to worry about, but the memories of her previous flight were returning and a sick feeling in her stomach was making her want to turn and run. She spun around as she heard footsteps approach and came face to chest with her captain and friend, Chuck Wallis, who towered above her.

He greeted her, embracing her and kissing her cheek. 'Maggie, it's good to see you!'

He grinned as he signalled towards the jet, 'Exciting isn't it?'

Maggie forced a smile and nodded.

It was exciting, everything was exciting. It was 1961 and Maggie was an air hostess working out of London Airport; travelling to places that most people would only see on postcards. This year brought new aircraft and a new terminal would be opening soon, opening the world up to a new generation of travellers. Maggie had always found the airport to be an exciting place. She was part of an exclusive group of young women that many longed to join. She felt the same tingle on her hundredth flight as she had on her first day, but not today. Maggie looked the part with her model figure; tall, slim and blonde, but her last flight had changed her. Although outwardly she was smiling, inside she felt like that small girl, hiding in the cupboard, desperate not to be found.

It was clear from the smell and the spotless cabin that the plane had never been occupied by passengers. Maggie knew she should be delighted to be a part of this adventure. New aircraft meant new routes and new places to explore.

Shaking herself, she stowed her bags as the rest of the crew joined them, all pleased to see her back at work.

Donna, their purser for the day, said, 'Right ladies, remember this is a historic moment. You have all been specially selected for this trip. We should arrive in Stockholm around 1pm, board the Royal Ballet and then it's a 2.5-hour flight back. Treat them like royalty, and if you need help with the language, we have Maggie here.' They all nodded, struggling to contain their excitement.

'Ready for this?' Chuck asked, leaning out the cockpit door and addressing Maggie who had made her way to the front galley. He was unsure what to say to his friend and sensed the uneasiness she was feeling.

'Take me home,' she smiled, indicating the sky.

*

As she sat looking out of the windows during their flight, listening to the chatter of her colleagues, she thought about her words to Chuck. Take me home. She sighed, wondering where that was. She felt London had only ever been a base for her adventures. Although for a time she considered that she would marry and remain there, the attraction was to her fiancé, not London itself. The more she thought, the more she realised the skies had been the only place she felt she truly belonged, but now even here, flying at 30 000 feet, she was lost.

*

Landing in Stockholm, the weather seemed to have followed them. Dark clouds hung over the airfield as heavy rain lashed the aircraft. Maggie breathed out, relieved to be back on the ground. Part of her was considering walking away from the plane, wondering if it was a possibility, wondering if the rest of the crew would notice, or try to stop her. Since her arrival in London seven years earlier, she had never considered returning to Sweden, but now that she was here, and given her realisation that the skies no longer felt like home, she couldn't shake the idea of just walking down the stairs and away from this life. She had done it before, and there was nothing to keep her in London. She was lost in her daydream when she heard the sound of footsteps on the aircraft stairs. The moment was gone.

'Welcome on board,' Donna greeted the passengers as Maggie counted them, and directed them down the aisle. She relaxed as she was able to do what she enjoyed most, talking to people. As the passengers shuffled to their seats, they chatted amongst themselves. She stood, listening as they spoke, catching bits of conversations and smiling, the sound of the language bringing back memories and distracting her from her thoughts.

'Is that the lot?' she asked Donna

'It seems to be, what was the number?'

'eighty-one passengers.'

'eighty-one is correct.' Donna nodded. 'Let's close up and roll out.'

Maggie looked down the aisle at the passengers, sensing their excitement and wondering if she would ever feel that way again. Taking her seat, she held onto her false smile as she accepted, she would be returning to London.

*

When they were in the air, Maggie loaded her trolley with newspapers, practising her smile before pushing it into the aisle.

'Something to read, Sir?' She began her trip through the aircraft, happy to be speaking Swedish again and enjoying the reaction she was getting. It was a good distraction, even if it did take her double the time it should have done as she explained several times about how she had moved to London in her teens. Sadly, no she had not been home in some time but certainly yes, she would love to visit again.

After leaving for London, she vowed never to return, desperate to get away from her old life. Now as she answered the questions, she realised there may be some truth in her answers. Perhaps it would be nice to return, or perhaps it was just the idea of leaving London she liked. She wondered if she was destined to live this way, always looking for the next escape.

As she reached the rear of the cabin, she nodded to her colleagues, before turning. She stopped part of the way down the aisle when she noticed the look on the face of their captain as he stood in the front galley, speaking in hushed tones with Donna, whose face was stern.

Taking a deep breath, she pushed her trolley to the front, feigning confidence whilst her legs shook. She knew that look on Chuck's face. She had seen it before, on the face of the last captain she worked with, not long before their plane crashed just short of the runway in Rome.

'What's happening?' she demanded, her smile gone as she entered the galley.

Chuck paused, pinching his forehead with his hand, thinking of how to explain what was happening in a way that wouldn't cause alarm.

'We're having a slight. . .' he paused, '. . .technical problem with the autopilot.' He kept his head low, unsure of how Maggie might react.

She paused for a moment, the colour draining from her face as she chewed on her lip, trying to hide her feelings. Her mouth was dry, her head was spinning. This couldn't be happening again, it had to be another dream. She closed her eyes momentarily but opened them again as the screams filled her mind.

'And what is our plan, Captain?' she said

'We are diverting to Berlin. We should be on the ground soon, there is a team there who can look her over and we'll be back in the air in no time.'

'You sound optimistic,' she responded as Donna turned to face her, surprised by the way she addressed her superior.

Chuck, who had been friends with Maggie since her first flight three years earlier, took no notice. He couldn't begin to imagine what was going on in her head, he wanted to reassure her, to remind her that he and the first officer were experienced pilots, but so was her last crew. He knew his assurances would do nothing to calm her nerves.

'I am. Listen to me, Maggie,' he said, holding her shoulders and looking her in the eye. 'This time it's different. There's no fire, just a glitch. We are going to be fine. Now, I need you to help Donna prepare the cabin for landing. You're the only one here who speaks Swedish, I need you to reassure the passengers. Okay?'

'Yes, Captain,' she answered, her voice shaking.

'Hey, come on, you're finally getting to Berlin!' He tried to joke, before returning to the flight deck.

Maggie fought to retain her composure as the plane bumped and shook in the unsettled air on its approach to Berlin.

She sat straight up in her seat, feet flat on the ground, ready to dive across and throw the door open should anything go wrong. She looked up the cabin, the passengers appeared calm, smiling at each other and pointing out the window, unaware of the danger they were in. No one on board seemed to understand the danger they were in.

They had faith in Chuck and were comforted by his words. They didn't have the sick feeling rising in their stomach that Maggie had right now, and for the second time that day, she envied them. Envied how they felt, they had hope.

As the plane descended, Maggie listened closely to the pilots, catching a few words through the door. They sounded composed, and she closed her eyes. When she opened them the cabin had changed. It was darker, not from the storm, but from thick black smoke that rolled along the aisles and ceilings. The previously calm passengers appeared lifeless. Their dead eyes open, staring at her, full of fear and anger. Maggie breathed in but instead of inhaling air, her lungs were filled with smoke, burning her throat and causing her to cough. Instinctively she leaned forward, closing her eyes.

*

'Maggie. Maggie!' Donna hissed.

Her eyes shot open, looking at her colleague as she continued to cough.

'Now is not the time,' she scolded.

'Sorry,' Maggie whispered as the feeling in her throat released. 'I'm fine.'

'Hm,' Donna responded. 'Just stay calm. Remember where you are.'

Maggie nodded looking back towards her door, realising they were almost on the ground.

The plane landed with a gentle bump. There was no screech of metal on the ground, no roar of the fire as the jet fuel set alight, there was nothing unusual. The passengers cheered as they looked out of the windows. They were on the ground. They were safe for now.

'Ladies and Gentlemen, welcome to Berlin,' Chuck's voice filled the cabin as the plane rolled to a halt. 'Please take this time to stretch your legs, your crew will be happy to direct you, however, we ask at this time that you do not venture too far from the aircraft to allow a speedy departure and reduce further delays.'

Most of the passengers were happy to stay on board, however, a number began to filter down the steps, braving the rain.

'May I borrow Maggie?' Chuck asked.

'Sure,' she nodded, signalling for Maggie to follow him.

Chuck looked around to ensure no one was listening.

'I just wanted to check you're okay.'

'I'm fine, you don't need to check up on me.'

'C'mon, you hide it well, but I know you, we've worked closely for a long time now. An emergency landing, and I know you have a thing about Germany...'

He paused as she scowled, breathing deeply but not speaking.

'That's you,' a voice interrupted from the cockpit as the engineer appeared smiling. 'Simple fix, not uncommon on this type. You are good to go.'

Chuck looked back at Maggie.

'I guess we better fly then.' She said, turning to alert the passengers who had disembarked.

*

Maggie looked at her watch. It wouldn't be long now until they arrived in London. In the months when she wasn't flying, she longed to be back at work, to be back in the skies, but today she was realising the love she had was gone. It died in the crash.

Donna's voice cut across her thoughts. 'Maggie, I hope you don't think I'm being rude, but are you okay to work? Do you feel ready to be back?'

'I was a little shaken, but I am fine, given the circumstances...' she began.

'Good. Then a word of advice, remember where you are. No disappearing for cosy chats with the captain when you should be working.'

Confused by Donna's attitude change, Maggie frowned. She was preparing to defend herself when she heard a ding!

Saved by the bell, she thought

'I'll go,' she muttered, turning to follow the sound.

Walking up the aisle, Maggie located the call bell and stopped smiling.

Sitting in front of her was a man she had never seen before. Maggie frowned, looking around her as the man smiled back, a warm kind smile, seemingly oblivious to the way she was looking at him.

'Hello, Miss, please may I have a glass of water? I missed you last time.' The man spoke clear English with an accent, which she recognised instantly as German.

Frozen to the spot, Maggie looked him over. He was older, maybe in his late 50s, wearing a brown suit with a green tie and brown hat to match. He had a pair of gold glasses perched on his nose, and she was sure they were there for show. He had a moustache and a warm smile that reminded her of someone, she just couldn't think who. He had a newspaper on his knee and Maggie knew she had not given it to him, nor had she seen this man board in Sweden. Around them, everyone acted normally, unaware of the sudden appearance of the passenger.

'Um yes, water. I'll be right back, Sir,' she managed. She walked to the rear of the aircraft to avoid Donna.

'Everything alright, Maggie?' One of her colleagues asked as she reached the galley.

'Sure,' she lied, as she pored the water. 'It's just, the passenger in row 12. I don't remember seeing him until now.'

Bev peered down the aisle and shrugged. 'No one came on in Berlin.'

'Are you sure? I mean no one passed me at the front, but I know I haven't seen him.'

'Maybe he didn't have his hat on before.' Bev responded, raising her eyebrow at their other colleague.

Maggie nodded, realising they were doubting her.

As she moved through the aircraft, Maggie looked at the rows of passengers. Nothing in this man's appearance matched any of the others within the dance group, everything about his appearance made him stand out, she knew he did not belong.

'Your water, Sir.' She smiled, placing the glass in front of the mystery man.

'Thank you.' He nodded.

Maggie stood, unsure what to say, but knowing she had to say something.

'Are you enjoying your flight?'

'Much better than the last one I was on, I must say.'

'May I fetch you anything else?'

'No, I am content.' He smiled, in the manner of a grandparent to a grandchild.

Despite his warmth, something in what he said, and his sudden appearance unnerved her. She was sure there was more to this man. Reaching into his pocket he retrieved a gold pocket watch, she frowned as she looked at the time, six fifty-five.

'You should prepare yourself, Maggie. It's almost time.'

'Sorry, time for wha—' she began as the PA system crackled, and Chuck announced they would be arriving in London soon.

Maggie hurried down the aisle towards a bewildered Donna.

'There is another passenger on board who isn't with the dance group.'

'Sorry? What?'

'Row 12. The passenger who asked for the water. He must have sneaked onto the plane. He is not Swedish, and he did not board in Sweden.'

'Are you sure?'

'Yes, I am sure!'

'Why would he draw attention to himself by calling you?'

'I don't know, I am telling you I have not seen him before!'

Donna sighed with frustration as she opened the cockpit door speaking to the pilots.

'What's going on?' Chuck asked as he entered the galley.

'We have an extra passenger,' Maggie blurted out before Donna could reply.

'You're sure?'

'Yes!'

Chuck raised his hands in defence. 'We are getting ready to begin final descent. We need to establish what is happening now. Do a headcount then report back.'

Both nodded, moving through the cabin counting.

'eighty-one...eighty-two...' Maggie reached the galley, her stomach somersaulting as Donna stopped behind her.

'eighty-one. There's eighty-one. Agreed?'

'I counted eighty-two.'

Donna sighed, exasperated. 'There's nothing unusual happening here Maggie, I understand you are shaken, but I can count. There are eighty-one passengers. I will speak with Captain Wallis. Now prepare the cabin for landing.'

Maggie opened her mouth to speak as Donna disappeared towards the cockpit. She blinked back tears of frustration, sure she was right, there was an extra passenger.

As the passengers began disembarking, Chuck made his way out of the cockpit.

'Always looks good if the captain puts in an appearance,' he said, winking at Maggie as she was forced to step aside into the galley.

She sighed, sure that the only reason he had taken the position was to keep her away from the passengers.

*

Exhausted by the day's events, Maggie exited the terminal building back into the grey London afternoon. She was enjoying breathing in the fresh air when she spotted a familiar figure standing a few feet away looking lost.

'May I help you, Sir?' She spoke, her voice sharp, less friendly than it should have been. She was no longer on duty, but she was in uniform. Nevertheless, she was tired and irritated from her day.

'Ah, Maggie!' The man responded, greeting her as if she were a friend, either unaware of her tone or choosing to ignore it. This unsettled her further.

'Could you tell me how to get to central London?' he asked.

'Shouldn't you be with your group?'

'Group? I think you must have mistaken me for someone else. I have simply visited the airport to take some photographs, I heard there was a new aircraft arriving today. You will show me the way, yes?' He spoke enthusiastically waving his camera around.

Maggie stood partly stunned, but also intrigued at the calmness in his voice as he lied to her. She was trying to think of what to say next when she heard another voice behind her.

'Hey! Maggie!' Chuck appeared through the door she had just exited from. 'Can I give you a lift?'

His eyes were low, he knew she was angry with him after what had happened with the supposed mystery passenger, but she was his friend, and he was concerned for her.

Turning to face him, Maggie glanced between him and the mystery man. The coolness in the way he spoke unnerved her, yet something about him felt warm and friendly, even though she knew he was lying. She should turn and leave, but she couldn't do it. Part of her wanted to find out more about the passenger, the other was mad at Chuck for the way he sided with Donna and dismissed her concerns. As was typical for Maggie, her stubborn side won, even if she knew it was not the most sensible choice.

'No, thank you, I have business in the city to tend to.' She smiled at Chuck who looked uneasy as he looked past her.

Maggie turned back towards the man who had turned his back and was watching a flight take off in the distance, almost hopping with excitement at the world around him.

'You sure? 'Chuck replied.

'Thank you. We have a bus to catch.' She spoke, moving away from him before he could change her mind.

'Let's go, Mister....'

'Winter.' He smiled, continuing to look around, fascinated by his surroundings. His face was soft, his eyes wide and his reaction to where they were interested Maggie further.

'We?' Chuck muttered, his heart sank as he watched his friend walk off towards the bus stance.

*

'Isn't this lovely?' Mr Winter declared, looking around the bus. Lovely wasn't the word Maggie would have used to describe it. It was battered, old, with torn leather on the some of the seats that had been taped together and a smell of dampness in the air. It was mostly empty with only a few other passengers sitting close to the front of the vehicle. Maggie had directed her new acquaintance to sit at the rear of the bus, knowing this may be her only chance to work out who he was. She watched him, desperate to speak but not wanting to ruin his fun.

'So, who are you?' She demanded; her voice louder than she had intended. She looked down the aisle, but none of the other passengers seemed to have noticed them.

'I am simply a man on a bus, with a lovely young lady for company. Who are you?'

Maggie breathed deeply, trying to remain calm. As fascinating as she was finding him, he was also very frustrating.

'This is not a simple situation, and you know that.'

'Perhaps not. But it could be. It could be just a moment. Just an old man and a young woman travelling on a bus, sharing a moment before going our ways. Wouldn't that be nice?'

'I guess, but it wouldn't be honest, would it?' She paused, wondering what to say, how to get the reaction she wanted. 'I could tell the police. Report you if I chose to.'

Mr Winter continued to look out the window, gasping at the scenery and smiling to himself.

Finally turning to face Maggie, he answered 'You could, but you won't.'

'What makes you so sure of that?'

'Because we all have our secrets, and you are not who you say you are, isn't that right?'

Maggie's face turned red as she stared at the man who sat beside her. His expression hadn't changed, his smile was still friendly, but she knew that was a threat and now her head was swirling wondering why she had put herself in danger. She wanted to get off the bus, but she didn't want to draw attention to them, hoping that they could get to the city and quietly go their separate ways, hoping he would not follow her, or worse, cause her harm.

'How?' She managed, her voice wavering as she tried to hold back tears.

Mr Winter reached down, taking her hand which was shaking.

'You wouldn't believe me if I told you.' A look of concern on his face as he studied Maggie. 'I am not here to cause you trouble, nor do I wish you any harm. I merely want to get to London. To safety. I have my own business to attend to, and should you wish, you need never see me again. But please, Maggie, do not cause trouble for me. It will only bring danger to you, and I do not wish for you to be brought into my troubles.'

Unsure of what to say she nodded, looking at his hand as it held hers, looking at the difference in them, her own dainty with soft skin and perfect nails, his rough, the skin rough to touch.

Their eyes met as Maggie tried to compose herself.

He continued, 'I am like you. I am lost, in need of a home. Alone.' He squeezed her hand before letting it go. Her head reeled, trying to work out how he seemed to know her inner thoughts and her darkest secrets.

He nodded, seemingly answering some question in his mind as he checked his pocket watch which still read the same time six fifty-five.

As the bus rolled into central London, he exclaimed, 'Aha, look at that! Ah to see it up close, it's ..., it's ..., it's beautiful don't you think?'

Maggie didn't answer, but he seemed happy again, and she wondered where he had been if he thought this was beauty, but she dared not to ask any further questions, fearful of the response.

Before long, the bus pulled into Victoria Coach Station. Stepping down onto the tarmac, Maggie became aware of how busy the station was. People, mostly men, rushed in various directions, most of them with long coats, buttoned up to keep out the autumn wind that was currently whistling through the open doorways of the station. She presumed they were commuters, travelling home, travelling alone with a briefcase in hand, newspapers under their arm that they had picked up from the stand that was just outside the main entrance, and the same serious look on their faces. For a second, Maggie became lost in her thoughts, wondering what it must be like to have a normal job, to travel to the same place at the same time each day, to see the same faces before returning home again. She shivered. The skies might not feel like home right now, but that life certainly did not sound appealing either.

'Well, Maggie, I believe this is goodbye.' Mr Winter nodded, tipping his hat as he did.

'Yes, I believe so. It's been...' She stopped, trying to think of the word when she noticed a dark change in his face for the first time as he looked around him.

'What is it?' she asked.

'Nothing for you to concern yourself with. You have done enough already.'

She sighed. 'Tell me. Perhaps I can help.'

Mr Winter nodded, still distracted by something that was not obvious to Maggie.

'There is a man, by the door, wearing a black coat and red bow tie. Do you see him?' He spoke in hushed tones, his words hurried. Maggie didn't speak, only nodded. 'And another at that exit. They are expecting me. I don't know how they know I am here, but if he sees me, I will not be safe. I will be dead; you are in danger by speaking with me. You must go now.'

'And you?'

'I accepted this may happen. Do not worry.'

Without thinking, Maggie started to walk towards the first man that Mr Winter had pointed out.

'Move now!' she said as she marched across the concourse, her heart beating faster as she went.

'Mr James?' She spoke, as she approached the man, her voice loud and friendly.

The man in the bow tie turned to look at her, taken aback by her sudden appearance.

'I am sorry, Miss, I don't know a Mr James. You are mistaken.'

'Oh no, don't tell me I have missed him. I am always running late! I hope they don't fire me over this one,' she said, keeping his attention.

'Sorry, Miss...' he began again.

Maggie waved her hand, trying to keep his focus on her for a moment longer, hoping that she was distracting him for long enough.

'It's not your fault, entirely my mistake. I will leave you to get on with your day.'

The man frowned as he stared at her, his eyes were a deep shade of green and she noticed his accent was English. She had expected German at least. They stood at the same height, face to face, Maggie sure to look him in the eyes to stop him from spotting her new friend in the crowds that moved towards the street outside.

'No, it's no problem...' He began again, as Maggie glanced out into the rain, watching Mr Winter as he disappeared into the crowd.

'Never mind,' she cut across him again. The man frowned, becoming impatient with her. 'I see a friend in the street. Sorry to have bothered you. Have a lovely day.' She smiled, stepping back, ready to turn towards the exit.

'Not so fast, Miss.' Came a voice from behind her as felt a hand grip her wrist. The man, whom she presumed was the second one that had been pointed out to her, moved closer.

'The man you have travelled here with is very dangerous. I need you to tell me where he went.'

Maggie held her breath as the grip on her wrist tightened.

'I... I don't know what you're talking about. I'm looking for a Mr James.' She managed; her voice not as quiet as she would have liked.

'What are you doing, William?' Spoke the man in the bow tie, frowning at his colleague and the way he was handling the young woman who had approached him.

William ignored the question, continuing to tighten his grip on Maggie. He stood in a way that hid his action from any curious passers-by.

'Oh, I think you do know, you know very well who I am talking about. Now, you seem nice, and I don't want to hurt you, Miss. Don't want to, but I will if I have to.' He growled, his voice low, as Maggie flinched from the pain he was inflicting on her. The man in the bow tie shifted uncomfortably as he watched her struggle, but did not speak, continuing to look around him, ensuring they weren't attracting any unwanted attention.

'Now start talking. Where is the German?'

A tear ran down Maggie's cheek, and she looked around, hoping someone might notice, but everyone else continued to walk by, hurrying about their day. She thought hard, wondering what to say, hoping for rescue, but scared of the consequences if she called out or tried to run.

*

From the street Mr Winter breathed out, relieved to feel the air on his face. He checked his watch then looked back towards the station when he spotted Maggie.

'No,' he said out loud, his voice full of anger and despair at being so close to escaping. His shout caused the man beside him to turn and stare. Winter glanced around him, knowing he could disappear into the crowd, knowing this was his chance for freedom, but also knowing he couldn't do it.

He headed back towards the station, as he walked, he freed the blade he had been concealing in the lining of his jacket. He had hoped not to need it, to avoid attention, but Maggie had risked her life for him without knowing him and he could do nothing.

*

'You know they say this is sharp enough to cut through bone,' Winter whispered, as he appeared behind them, and held the blade against the man with the bow tie. He leaned on his shoulder and positioned the blade against his neck, doing his best to ensure it was hidden from the view of passers-by.

'Now, I don't know if that's true for something so small, but if you don't let my friend go, I am willing to find out.'

At the appearance of Mr Winter, William let go of Maggie, pushing her to the side towards the crowds of people, as he reached for his pistol.

Maggie looked towards Mr Winter. He was outnumbered, his eyes were tired, but he nodded to her as he pressed the blade against the man's neck, causing a small trickle of blood to run down towards his bow tie.

Maggie was frozen, she needed to run, but she couldn't leave. She knew she needed to cause a distraction. Fire? No, without smoke they would just keep walking by. Maggie was panicking, looking at her new friend, desperately trying to think of a solution.

'BOMB!' She yelled suddenly as loud as she could, the crowd around her stopped momentarily, confused, not sure where the voice had come from.

'That man has a bomb in his briefcase! Get out! Get out! Evacuate!' She shouted, in the manner that she was trained to evacuate an aircraft.

'Did she say bomb?'

'What?'

She heard the murmurs spread in the crowd as panic set in. Within seconds, the word bomb was rippling through the busy group as people began pushing towards the exit where Mr Winter stood, pushing into him and the two men, moving them towards the street, as the panicked commuters rushed to get out. Maggie lost sight of them as she ducked into the crowd, trying to escape before one of the policemen who were trying to control the panic caught up with her. She closed her eyes as she felt herself being carried along as hundreds of people moved in the same direction, then within seconds, she felt the cold air hit her as they spilt onto the street.

Glancing around her, she could not see anyone familiar as she tried to decide which way to go, still moving with the large crowd. She knew she had to leave. She wanted to know if Mr Winter was safe, but she was sure the men would hold her captive as a bargaining tool if he had escaped, she couldn't risk waiting around. She tried to disguise herself as she walked, pulling her hat from her head and donning her coat over her uniform.

Maggie thought back to her dream that morning.

'Greta, we know you're here.'

She gulped. Maybe it had been a warning.

*

The rain continued as daylight began to fade in the cold evening. Maggie tried to control her breathing and rid herself of the sense she was being watched. She knew she needed to head for Victoria train station but had walked in the opposite direction that she would normally go; fearful that she was being followed.

She was almost at Sloane Square when she sensed someone walking beside her, keeping pace, she glanced to the side as she felt the man link arms with her.

The voice of Mr Winter arrived in her ear. 'Good job, Maggie. I cannot thank you enough. I wanted to make sure you weren't followed. You are safe.' He continued to walk with her, arm in arm as he talked. He spoke quickly, yet with a strange calm considering what had just happened. She wanted to cry, but she knew she needed to keep moving.

'Who are you?' Maggie asked again, not sure what to expect given his earlier response. 'Do not say simply a man.'

'Does it matter who I am?' Just know that I will not forget what you have done for me today.'

A shiver ran down Maggie's spine, something in the way he said it made her realise that perhaps those seeking him were quite right to be doing so.

'Tell me the truth. Are you the bad guy, or are they?'

'That's a matter of perspective.' Mr Winter sighed as he briefly met Maggie's gaze before fiddling with his pocket watch, which she was sure was still showing six fifty-five.

Glancing back towards the sky, he thought out loud. 'I used to believe in good and evil, but the truth is people aren't all good or all bad. Sometimes, it is not so simple. It's not black and white, we're all just different shades of grey and some people are darker inside than others.'

He smiled back at Maggie, a weaker smile this time, signalling to her that for the first time since they met, he was giving her a truly honest answer.

'I guess that includes me too doesn't it?' she responded, thinking about her own life.

'Ah, Maggie. You are just a little bit silver. It's why you sparkle! Now, this time, we must say goodbye and I must work out where to go next. I hadn't expected to reach this point!' He laughed to himself. 'So much of me wants to just walk, to see London, however, time is drawing on and I would prefer not to spend my first evening sleeping on the streets. Tell me do you know of any where worth staying?'

'You came to London with no plan of what to do? That seems rather….'

'Adventurous! Don't you think?' He smiled in a way that lit up his face. 'Or perhaps you were thinking familiar, for is that not what you did?'

Maggie pulled her arm away sharply, breaking free of his grip, alarmed by this new revelation. Questions were running through her mind, although she was learning that he would not answer them in any sensible manner. She tried to think fast, wondering how this man knew so much, wondering if he was playing some sort of game with her if he was reading her mind.

'I know a place. It's not too far from here. It won't offer you much, just a bed, but it is comfortable. All I ask is that you promise to keep trouble away from their door.' She was unsure if she was making the right decision as she let her impulsive side take over.

'Wonderful! Lead the way!'

*

As they turned the corner into a familiar lane, they stopped outside the boarding house that she had stayed in when she first arrived in London. She had been a scared teenager with very little money, and a basic understanding of English. Mrs Wells, the owner, had taken Maggie under her wing, teaching her and then supporting her to find employment. A widow, with no family of her own, they became each other's family and despite the many friendships Maggie had built over the years, Mrs Wells was the only person she truly trusted.

The space felt smaller than it had before, and she noticed the unpleasant smell that hung in the air as a result of the water that ran down the buildings and across the cobbles.

'Maggie Sommaren!' exclaimed Mrs Wells as she opened the door. She was dressed in her usual dark dress and apron. Judging by the mess, Maggie was sure she had been baking. 'Look at you, my girl! Not a girl anymore!' She smiled rushing forward to hug the woman whom she treated as one of her own.

'What brings you this way of a Tuesday evening?' she asked, suddenly aware that they were not alone.

'May I come in?'

'Always. You know that.' She eyed Mr Winter curiously, although he appeared not to notice. He laughed to himself, looking up at the buildings that rose above his head. He remained on the doorstep while the two women disappeared into the house.

A few moments later, Maggie exited with keys in her hand which she pressed into his palm.

'Your room is at the very top of the house, rent is to be paid to Mrs Wells weekly. Please don't upset her, I am trusting you, although I do not know why. No noise after 10 pm, clean up after yourself and no visitors.'

Mr Winter chuckled to himself. 'I am a little too old for that.'

He looked at Maggie, his smile slipping, his eyes looking tired, the spark dulling slightly. 'You have put your trust in me. I will not let you down.'

'It has been my pleasure, Mr Winter. And if you are here, perhaps we shall meet again.'

'Oh please, call me Max!' He smiled.

'Max?' Maggie whispered, the colour draining from her face as she put her hand against the building to steady herself. He moved forward, holding her up.

'Perhaps you should sit for a moment.' He appeared to be unsurprised by her reaction.

*

The door of the flat clicked shut behind her as Maggie dropped her keys onto the table. She had slipped one shoe off when her two flatmates came tumbling out into the hallway.

'Maggie! Where on earth have you been?' demanded Betty. She was the oldest of the three friends as well as the tallest thanks to the elaborate way she fixed her black hair on top of her head.

'Work,' Maggie replied flatly. She indicated her uniform as she removed her other shoe and began taking her coat off, hanging it up as the water ran off onto the floor.

'You should have been home hours ago!'

'That pilot friend of yours has been calling for hours now.' chimed in Julie, whose expression was less serious than Betty's.

'You know the one, the dashing American guy, Chuck? How is that man still single?'

Betty silenced her. 'Julie!"

She turned her attention back to Maggie. "He said you went off with some stranger and then you don't come home for hours, it's almost 9 pm Maggie, we were about phone the police.'

'I'm fine. A passenger was in a bit of a situation, I helped them out. That was all.'

'What kind of situation?'

Maggie sighed as she looked at her two friends. Betty her face serious, was taking on the role of mother, Julie - who loved hearing Maggie's tales from her travels - was excited to hear the story, sure it was a good one.

'He came to London, didn't know where he was going, had nowhere to stay. He...appeared on the flight. I don't know how but he was lost, he needed help. It's weird though, he knew things about me...'

'He could have done anything to you, Maggie!' Betty interrupted, her patience for her friend wearing thin after hours of imagining her being led to her death.

'How did you know he wasn't a murderer? Or a spy? Or a...a..'

'Communist?' Julie chimed in.

'I didn't. I still don't.' Maggie shrugged. 'But I know he knows things about me, things that neither of you would know. And his name is Max.'

The two friends shot a worried look at each other, neither of them knowing what to say when the phone interrupted their conversation.

'Oh, hi Chuck. Yeah, no need, she's here. Yeah, hang on.'

Taking the receiver from Julie, Maggie waited until her friends had shuffled back into the lounge before she began her conversation with Chuck. He sounded relieved to hear her voice.

'I don't understand why you were so worried. You told me there was no mystery passenger. All in my imagination that's what you thought,' Maggie said. She was tired and angry at him for telling Betty; knowing that her friend wasn't going to let this go.

'I know. I'm sorry, I was under a lot of pressure you know that; the airline wanted to avoid any negative publicity, especially on the maiden voyage of a new jet. We'd already had the tech issue, can you imagine if they thought we let someone on? There's no way I could take that risk...'

'Ah, but you could risk letting a stranger into the country. Makes sense.'

Silence fell between them. Chuck knew she was right.

'Where is he now?'

'How should I know?' Maggie lied. 'I took him to London, we went our separate ways and I, as I told you earlier, I had business to tend to.'

Chuck thought for a moment, sure she wasn't telling him the whole story, but aware she was tired and annoyed.

'Meet me tomorrow at 11 am. There are some things I need to talk to you about. Usual place?'

Maggie agreed, before collapsing onto her bed. Her mind was still filled with thoughts of her day, and Mr Winter and Max.

*

The storm from the previous day had passed over. Maggie sat on the park bench enjoying the warmth of the sun as she waited for Chuck. She hadn't slept much as she continued to obsess over Mr Winter's identity and the men in the station, wondering if she was still in danger. She had already decided she wasn't going to share what happened at the bus station with anyone, not Julie, not Betty and certainly not Chuck.

When he arrived, she continued to look down at the city and wondered where Mr Winter was at this moment. She ignored her friend who sat, uncomfortable with the silence.

'You're not telling me something. I know you, Maggie, what's going on?'

'It's complicated. You wouldn't understand.'

'Give me a try at least? I know the past few months have been hard, since Max... since the accident. But I'm worried about you. Running off with a stranger, without a thought for your safety.' He raised his hand defensively before Maggie could speak, her cheeks reddening.

He continued, 'I know, I know what you're going to say, but I was in an awkward position, you know that. What could I have done?'

'Stood up for me? I don't know what the problem is with Donna, she doesn't like me, but you let her make it out like I was crazy! You took her word for it and you were wrong, you were so wrong.'

'I know. I should have listened, but you have no idea how much pressure I was under. We were already late, the press was waiting, I had to do what was best.'

'Best for who? Who knows who that man was?'

'Donna said there was only eighty-one when she counted, I counted myself as they left, and I got the same.'

'Maybe she was in on it, maybe she was helping him.' Maggie shrugged, looking away from Chuck.

'Oh, so am I in on it too?'

Maggie didn't respond, simply raising her eyebrow and returning her look towards the city.

'You don't believe that. What's on your mind?'

'He knew things about me, things no one knows.'

'What things?' Chuck demanded, sitting up straight and looking at his friend who remained silent.

'Talk to me, Maggie. What's going on?'

'Honestly, I don't know. There are things I have never shared, that I cannot share, but he knew them. And the fact his name is Max. It's a sign.' She stood up, from the seat glancing towards Chuck who also jumped to his feet, surprised by her sudden movement.

'I'm sorry Chuck, I have to go. I need to work this out, it has to mean to something, the Max connection... it has to mean something.'

'Do you think that's a good idea? Don't you think you should just let this go?'

'Why? Because it suits you? Because you messed up and let goodness knows who into the country?'

Chucks face flushed red with Maggie's accusation.

'This man knows things about me. Things nobody should know, and you think I should forget about it? I can't do that.'

'Then tell me what he knows, and we can work this out together.'

Maggie shook her head. 'There are things I cannot share, even with you.'

'But if these things are putting you in danger, you've gotta trust me.'

'Not even Max knew.'

'Okay, but Max isn't here anymore, and he would have wanted me to protect you. You can't do it on your own.'

'Maybe not. But I was the only one that walked away from the crash. Maybe I am destined to do things on my own. Thank you for your concern, but I have to go now, I have to work this out. I'll call you soon but for now, you have to trust me.'

Chuck watched as his friend hurried away in the direction of the nearest tube station. He sighed as he realised that although Maggie had survived the crash, he had lost her, had lost them both. He wondered if she blamed him for calling in sick that day if she blamed him for losing Max. He watched as she moved in the distance, then started following her, careful to remain unseen.

*

'Oh, Maggie! Didn't expect you again so soon!' Mrs Wells greeted her as she stood nervously in the lane. 'If you're looking for your friend though, he's not here, went out early.'

'Oh,' Maggie responded, her face fell, unsure what her next step should be.

'You're welcome to come in and help with the dinner if you like.' Mrs Wells smiled, hiding her concern at the look on the younger woman's face.

'Thanks, but I have something I need to do.' She turned and headed back to the high street before Mrs Wells could protest.

Making her way along the bustling street, Maggie couldn't shake the feeling that she was being watched. It was early afternoon, the heat from the sun was giving the impression of a summer's day which was adding to her discomfort, and she regretted her choice of outer-wear. As always with London, the high street was busy, full of the noise from the traffic and the voices of people scuttling by, all headed in different directions, showing no interest in those around them. Maggie breathed out as she chose her steps carefully, looking for any sign of the eyes she was sure were watching her. As she took another step, a flash of red in the crowd caught her eye. A red bow tie.

Without a second thought, she turned sharply, walking down a side street that was lined with tables from several cafes trying to make the most of nice weather before the rain returned. The street was busy with very few empty tables. Maggie slowed, catching words from numerous conversations that were happening around her as she looked along the row of cafes. As she was deciding which one would best hide her, she felt a hand on her arm.

'Take a seat over there. We need to talk.' A voice said, close to her ear.

She sat where she was told. 'How did you know I was here?' she asked, stirring the cup of tea that Mr Winter had placed in front of her.

He smiled, setting his cup down and brushing away pastry flakes from his lips before whispering, 'I wanted to make sure you were safe. I am not the only one who is following you.'

'Red bow tie?'

'Pardon? Oh. No. Turn around slowly. Six tables back, my right.'

Maggie knocked her spoon to the ground, looking back as she picked it up.

'Chuck?' Maggie gasped, noticing her friend sitting, appearing to read a newspaper. She looked back at Mr Winter. 'No, he's my friend.'

'Your friend is following you. Maybe he is looking out for you. Or, more likely, he thought you would lead him to me.'

'You?'

'Maggie, you were right when you said I was not simply a man. There's more to this, there's more to all of this, and I can explain it to you.'

'Can you explain how you know so much about me?' she asked.

'Yes, I can. Just not here.'

'If I am being followed, why are we having tea?'

He grinned. 'No one wants to run on an empty stomach. You're right, someone else is watching, it is time we moved. I need you to trust me. You were right about the man with the red bow tie. Now pick up your cup, take it back to the counter and follow me. You understand?'

'And if I don't?'

'Then I cannot protect you. Your friend may help you, but if I were you, I would not presume he is loyal.'

Maggie frowned, taking in what he said. Mr Winter took out his pocket watch, sighing as he looked at the time which remained at six fifty-five.

'I need to move, now! Are you coming with me?' he asked, the fear in his eyes now evident as he looked over Maggie's shoulder to some unseen figure at her back.

'Okay, I will if you answer me one thing.'

'Which is?'

'You know things I haven't told anyone. Who told you all of this?' She placed her hands under the table to hide the fact they were shaking.

Mr Winter nodded, expecting the question. He knew the answer would raise more questions, but also that he had to tell her the truth.

'Well, who was it?'

'It was you, Maggie. You told me.'

As instructed, Maggie returned her cup to the counter then followed the mysterious man as he led her through the small kitchen, passed surprised staff out into a narrow lane.

'How did you?' Maggie began asking, signalling around them.

Mr Winter smiled in response, taking her hand and leading the way further into the darkness of the lane.

*

Chuck sat, looking at the vacant table where Maggie had been moments before, waiting for her to return to the street. He tapped his fingers on the table, becoming impatient, when he noticed the other man pass close by, staring at the empty table. He walked towards the cafe door, the colour of his face changing.

Chuck only caught a few words from one side of the conversation. 'A man and woman. Just came through here. I saw them. No, it wasn't another cafe. It's a matter of national security!'

The stranger finally gave up, running up the lane past Chuck, who caught a flash of red as the figure disappeared into the crowd behind him.

'What are you doing Maggie?' he grumbled, folding his paper and considering his next steps.

*

'How do you know where you are going?' Maggie asked, still being dragged along across cobbles.

'Not now. I'm thinking.' Mr Winter answered, looking around the labyrinth they had found themselves in.

Despite her years spent living in the city, Maggie was lost. The lanes felt never-ending as they made their way through the shadows cast by the tall buildings that rose on each side.

'Ah. This one!' The excitable German declared, opening a door in one of the brick walls that lined the narrow passageways they had been moving along.

Without stopping to think, Maggie stepped through the doorway, pausing as she realised he had led her into the storeroom of a shop. She waited on one of the workers to notice them, to shout, but as she followed the older man through onto the shop floor, no one acknowledged them, and within seconds, they were back out in the sunshine with people rushing by.

'We are safe for now. Let's find somewhere to talk.'

The air was starting to cool as they took a seat in Hyde Park, and for a few minutes, neither of them spoke.

'Who are you?' Maggie asked, breaking the silence. 'Are you a spy? Are you dangerous? Am I wrong to trust you?'

Silence fell between the pair as Mr Winter removed his glasses, rubbing the lenses on a handkerchief that he produced from his pocket. Putting his glasses back on his face, he folded the small fabric square, handing it to Maggie.

The letters M.W were stitched in the corner.

'This belonged to Max,' she gasped, her hand shaking. 'My Max, how did you..?' She trailed off, feeling light-headed.

Mr Winter reached over, place a hand on her back.

'Are you alright?'

She nodded, still looking at him, searching for answers.

'You gave me that, Maggie, the first time we met.'

'No, I met you yesterday, I lost this the same day I lost Max.'

Mr Winter did not speak, simply nodded his head, his eyes were full of sympathy for her, he knew what he had to say was going to cause her further pain.

'No, you couldn't have been there.' Maggie looked intently at his face as he took his pocket watch out, holding it for her to take.

Her gaze fell to the gold watch and as she lifted it from his hand, allowing it to sway gently on the chain, she remembered.

'This can't be,' Maggie gasped. 'You cannot have been on that flight; I am the only one who survived.' She raised her eyes to meet his. 'Are you a ghost?'

'No, not a ghost,' he responded, taking her hand as proof.

'Then are you a spy? Is your name even Max? How did you survive?'

He sighed, continuing to hold her hand.

'My name is Max, a strange coincidence. A spy? I don't know if you would say that. I have done things, bad things for bad people.' He thought for a second, choosing his words carefully. 'But I am not a bad man, Maggie, I just wanted my daughter to be safe. She was taken during the war, they told me she was still alive.' He paused, looking into the distance. 'They lied.'

'But nobody survived, just me.'

'We both survived. I don't know how, I should have died, but I didn't, and I sat with you, in the wreckage. I held your hand. That's when you told me, you thought you were dying. You told me about Greta, about your father, about how you escaped Germany.'

Maggie struggled to take in what he was saying. 'What is happening? Why are people following me? Why were you following me?'

'Today, I was following your friend, who was following you.'

'Chuck?'

'You cannot trust him, Maggie. Whatever you take from this, do not trust that man. Think about it, he knew there was another passenger and what did he do?'

Maggie frowned; tears of frustration formed in her eyes. 'This makes no sense.'

'Let me ask you this, do you think it is a coincidence that he was unable to work the day a plane falls from the sky?'

She opened her mouth, pausing as she realised the implications of what he said.

'No, it was an accident, there was a fire on board, it knocked out the hydraulics, they couldn't control the plane. It was an accident.' She sounded as if she was trying to reassure herself. 'Wasn't it?'

Mr Winter reached up with his left hand and removed his hat to reveal his hair that appeared whiter than the day before.

'It was no accident.'

'How can you be sure?'

'Because I am the one who set the fire. I am the reason the plane crashed.'

Silence fell between the pair as Maggie processed the words.

'No,' she managed feebly, her body shaking.

'Yes. There were people on board that flight, bad people, my job was to bring down the plane, make it look like an accident. They killed many people, thousands of people, and they were going to get away with it.'

As he spoke, Maggie could see tears in his eyes.

'But what about the rest of us? We didn't do anything.'

'I know, but I have seen so much death, so many innocent people died, and they had to be stopped, at any cost.'

'You killed my Max. You killed my friends.' Her voice rose slightly, attracting the attention of a few passersby, who raised their eyes before shuffling on.

'I know.'

'How can you say you are not a bad man?'

'Come on Maggie, you were there in Germany, you saw what happened, you were part of it. You know it is not that simple. Nothing in life is so simple. And with what your father did...'

'So, I am to be punished for something that happened when I was a child? How is that just?'

'You're not. It's not. I cannot tell you how sorry I am, but they told me they would hurt Lotti, and I did what they asked. Only I survived, and that's when I learned she was already dead.'

The silence between them returned, and Maggie realised she still had her hand in his. Forcefully removing it, she tried to work out her escape. She wanted desperately to get away from the man who had killed her fiancé, but she knew if he was being truthful, there was more to fear.

Either through nerves or habit, Mr Winter reached for his watch. Six fifty-five.

'Not much time,' he muttered to himself.

'What do you mean? You are going to hurt me, aren't you?'

He shook his head, his eyes heavy, full of sadness.

'What do you want to do with your life, Maggie?' He looked around the park apprehensively as if he sensed someone approaching.

'I...I... I don't know anymore,' she sighed. 'I wanted to travel the world, find love, have a family of my own.'

She stopped for a moment, looking him in the eye. 'But someone took that from me. Now, I guess, I want to live without fear.'

Mr Winter nodded. 'I thought that might be the case. After today, you will not see me again, make sure you do it. Live without fear.'

'If this is goodbye, then tell me why you were on my flight, how did you just come to be on a plane that was never supposed to be in Berlin, that I just happened to be on?'

Mr Winter continued to look around, causing the hair on the back of Maggie's neck to stand up. She sensed it too.

'There was no technical fault, so again, ask yourself why your friend said there was.' The focus was returning to his eyes, alerting Maggie to the fact there was danger around.

'The truth is, I boarded that flight in Stockholm. I have contacts in Stockholm. You see after Rome I had made my way there to safety. When I heard your airline was flying into Sweden, I knew it was a sign to come back to the UK and finish this. I just needed some time, some evidence to prove what had happened, but the more time I spend here, the more I am putting you in danger.'

'But there were eighty-two, I counted. I'm sure I'm right.'

'You are. There was another passenger who boarded in Berlin, but it was not me, and no, I do not know their intentions, but I believe your pilot friend will. And on that note, my friend, it is time we fly.'

Without warning, he leapt from the bench, grabbing Maggie by the hand and dragging her along the stone path heading towards the park gates.

'I can't keep running,' he said, as they continued marching along, 'I need to hand myself in or they will continue to hunt you. But you have two choices, you can keep running, leave London and get away from that friend of yours, or you confront him and find out what his part in this is. I would prefer the former, go somewhere new, start a new life and live without fear, although I feel you will do as you please.'

Maggie's face flushed red, partly through embarrassment and also a touch of anger.

'Who is the man who is hunting you? The one with the bow tie?'

'British Intelligence.'

'Didn't take too kindly to you taking down a British airliner and killing civilians?' Maggie retorted as they reached the park gates.

'No,' he responded, stopping and pulling her round to face him. 'They didn't want me living to tell the tale of how they had me bring down one of their planes to kill those on board. I knew no one would believe me, I thought about spending the rest of my days in hiding, but then I thought about Lotti, and I wanted people to know the truth. It was rather naive of me really to think I could hold the government to account.'

Mr Winter squeezed her hand as four men approached from different directions, two of them Maggie recognised from the bus station. She hadn't seen the others before but the way their eyes were fixed on her companion, she knew who they were.

'Here, take this,' Winter said, as he pressed the gold watch into her hand and taking a step back. 'As the poet Nicolas Jones once said – "Do not listen to the things I have told you, hear the secrets I could not keep." Or something like that. Farewell, Greta.'

As he stepped away from Maggie, he smiled, allowing his eyes one last twinkle before raising his hands in the air.

'I surrender,' he said, loud enough to be heard, whilst remaining calm as the men gathered round. Maggie lowered her head, hoping to disappear into the crowds that were now slowing to watch the unfolding drama.

Bang!

Turning back, she watched as the colour drained from Max's face, a deep red stain spreading out across his clean white shirt as his body fell to the stone, the blood running onto the street.

'No! He was surrendering!' She managed, her voice wavering.

'I think, Miss, it is time that you leave and forget anything you have seen,' a voice said into her ear, the unmistakable red bow tie visible in her peripheral vision. 'Leave now and we shall say no more.'

Maggie gulped, nodding as she slowly turned to leave, feeling for the watch that she had hidden in her coat pocket.

'It's almost time.'

*

Walking alone, she tried to hold back the tears that threatened to fall. Was she sad Mr Winter was dead when he had confessed to killing Max, and almost killing her? She wasn't sure. It was not the first time someone had been killed in front of her eyes, but she could not remember life before she left Germany. Her mind whizzed through everything that had happened, the flight, Berlin, Mr Winter, Max. Her head was spinning, she had been walking for what felt like hours, unsure where she was, but she realised she should head for the nearest tube station and home, but she had a hunch Chuck would be waiting for her.

*

'Back again? Not that it's not nice to see you, but is everything alright, Maggie?' Mrs Wells greeted the young woman on the doorstep.

She opened her mouth to speak, but before she could utter a word tears flooded down her face causing the older woman to scoop her up from the pavement, bring her into the kitchen and sit her at the table.

'What's wrong? Are you hurt?'

Maggie shook her head. 'Not me, but he's dead.'

'Who is?'

'Max. He's dead.'

Mrs Wells paused, looking at her friend, trying to choose her words carefully.

'I know, Maggie. I remember.'

'No! Not my Max. Mr Winter. He's dead. They shot him.' She sobbed, dropping her head onto the wooden table that took up most of the room, as Mrs Wells attempted to console her.

'Good,' came a voice from the adjacent room. There was no mistaking the brash American accent.

Maggie's face was red from crying as she looked up at the man she had trusted as a friend. Her body felt heavy, she was tired, and she knew she couldn't outrun Chuck, but she had to try. Slowly, she rose to her feet, her eyes on him, back to the door.

'What are you doing here?' she asked, stepping backwards.

'We're worried about you, Maggie,' came a voice from behind her.

Spinning around, she saw Mrs Wells moving to block her exit.

'What has he told you?'

'The truth,' responded Chuck as he stepped into the room beside them. 'That you're too trusting, that you're in way over your head. We want to help you, Maggie, I can help you.'

'No. You're part of this.' Her voice wavered as she tried to think of an escape.

'Says who? The elusive Mr Winter? Who, if you hadn't noticed, was a German. Not to be trusted.'

'And does that mean I too am not to be trusted?' Maggie snapped before she could stop herself. She stood instantly regretting her words, feeling the eyes on her.

Mrs Wells broke the silence. 'No, you came 'ere from Sweden.'

'True, but it is not where I was born,' Maggie answered, lowering her eyes as she turned to face her friend. 'I did not mean to lie.'

'No matter, it weren't any of my business anyway,' Mrs Wells said as she shrugged and forced a smile to hide the hurt she felt.

'So,' Maggie turned back to face Chuck, trying to appear stronger than she felt. 'What happens now? Do you turn me in for knowing too much? Or do you make me disappear?'

Chuck pinched his forehead as he took a deep breath in, stepping towards his friend. Holding her shoulders, he looked her in the eyes.

'I make you disappear.'

*

The sun hadn't long risen and Chuck stood in the orange glow that fell across the airfield, still troubled by the decisions he had been forced to make. He knew it wouldn't be long before people began searching for Maggie, her friends would soon notice her missing, the airline would ask questions and he couldn't be sure there weren't any further loose ends.

'Good morning,' greeted the owner of the Electra that Chuck had been standing beneath.

'Morning Alfred, thanks for doing this,' he began, hiding the nerves in his voice.

'No problem, I've been looking for an excuse to take her out,' he smiled, looking proudly at his aircraft. 'Just a few checks then we're ready to roll, just need my passenger.'

Chuck nodded, signalling to the passenger who sat in the front of the car.

As she looked across the airfield one last time, Maggie turned towards Chuck. Her eyes were heavy from the long night spent in Mrs Wells kitchen. She still felt uncomfortable knowing that Chuck knew all her secrets, but now she knew his, she knew who he worked for and she knew the truth, well most of it.

'I have a final question,' Maggie said avoiding Chuck's eye.

'Sure, I guess I owe you that.'

'Who was passenger eighty-two?'

Chuck sighed, scratching his head, 'They don't tell me that. Only what I need to know, and on that flight, I had to divert to Berlin, pick someone up and ask no questions.'

Maggie nodded, clutching her small bag that contained the essentials she needed for her new life.

'Was it worth it?' she asked, looking him in the eyes.

'I am so sorry for everything, if I could change things I would, but you don't get a choice. You know that Maggie when you're in, you can't get out, you can't choose the jobs you accept.' He paused, knowing this would be the last time they spoke. 'Can you forgive me?'

Maggie shook her head as she thought about what Mr Winter had said.

'I understand why you made your choices, you let Max and I work on the flight, knowing you had been warned to stay away and that we were in danger. For that, I can never forgive you.'

Chuck opened his mouth to speak as she turned, walking away from London for good.

*

Sitting on the steps of the Sacré-Couer, Maggie breathed out as she looked out across the city below. The sun had set, and lights were sparkling in every direction.

'Isn't it beautiful?' A voice from her side interrupted her thoughts.

'It is,' she smiled. 'It's breath-taking.'

'Do you live in Paris or are you visiting?' The man at her side asked as she continued to look into the distance.

'Haven't decided yet.'

The stranger laughed in response, 'Well, before I leave you to your decision, would you happen to know the time?'

Maggie nodded, reaching into her bag and removing the pocket watch that had been entrusted to her.

'It's 7 o'clock,' she smiled, watching the second hand as it ticked round.

'Thank you, Miss...'

'Greta. My name is Greta,' she answered, gulping as she finally looked towards the person who had stopped to speak with her.

'Welcome to Paris, Greta,' he smiled, straightened his red bow tie as he stood up and then disappeared into the crowd.

About the Authors

Jim Beck

Originally from Glasgow, Jim moved to Mauchline in 1986 with his wife and family and has lived there ever since.

He has been writing poetry since he was 19, although it is only since he retired he has seriously considered publishing any of his poems.

This came about when he joined an Indie Authors World Writing Group and came into contact with other like-minded people who enjoy reading and writing short stories and poetry.

He has published 3 books of poems, "Salar", "Seasons" and "Sailor" which are available on Amazon in e-book form and also in printed format by contacting the author at jimspoems@yahoo.com.

Margaret Duffy

Margaret Helen Duffy was born in Glasgow, in 1941, left school at 15, married at 22 and raised 4 wonderful children. Monosyllabic by her mid-30s from a diet of baby babble, she went to Glasgow University, graduated with an English and Philosophy degree, and taught English until offered early retirement.

A voracious reader of fiction and non-fiction, she started writing as therapy; crime novels laced with romance, short stories, and articles. Her first, completed, novel was long-listed in the Mslexia novel competition. According to her daughter her writing is helped by, 'her ability to look forward, her flair for writing, and a childlike sense of humour.'

Lyndsay Kelly

yndsay is a Support Worker who lives north of Glasgow with her husband and two sons. Before joining the group, she had never shared any of her writing. Since the group began, she has now completed a novel and working on a second which she hopes to publish one day.

Carolyn Mandache

Carolyn Mandache is an author and business owner living in Scotland. Her first novel, "Behind the Curtain" was inspired by her interest in Romania, where her husband Florin was born; a country she has come to think of as a second home. Researching for the book allowed her to learn more about Romanian history, culture and traditions. Carolyn's aim with that book is to provide an insight into what life was like "behind the Iron Curtain" not as historical fact but as fiction.

She has a BA in English Literature from the University of Strathclyde, and can speak Romanian at conversational level. The author enjoys travelling with her husband and children, with a particular soft spot for Spain... where she met Florin on holiday .

Claire Miller

Claire has been writing seriously since 2001. She is a published author of three children's books and The Story Creator. Her books are Pure Human City, a teenage book, I Can Create Stories, an interactive story creating book and I Can Create Stories (Story Edition), a smaller story creating book. The Choice, a teenage novel, her fourth book was released at the end of 2021 which was meant to be a 1000 word story and grew a bit!

She is passionate about helping children and adults gain confidence in themselves and their abilities through story creating workshops. Please get in touch with her if you'd like to know more about her workshops.

She loves diving into her imagination and creating stories and now considers herself a full-time, accomplished, professional writer. When she's not writing she loves to play the piano and take photographs.

Information on all her books and free activity sheets can be found at her website – www.clairemillerauthor.co.uk.

She can be contacted at info@clairemillerauthor.co.uk and can be found on Facebook and Linkedin as Claire Miller Author.

www.ingramcontent.com/pod-product-compliance
Lightning Source LLC
Chambersburg PA
CBHW011208190726
48288CB00013B/3372